Erotica
Short Stories
Vol. 27

DEEPEST
AND
DARKEST

10 SECRET DESIRE STORIES IN 1

JUST PLAIN BOB

WARNING

This book contains sexually explicit scenes and adult language. It may be considered offensive to some readers. This book is for sale to adults ONLY.

Please store your files wisely where they cannot be accessed by underage readers.

* * * * * * * * * * * * * * * * * * *

About the Publisher

4Fun Publishing, a member of **BLVNP Incorporated**, 340 S. Lemon #6200, Walnut CA 91789, info@blvnp.com / legal@blvnp.com

NOTE: Due to the highly emotional reaction of some people to works of erotic fiction, any email sent to the above address that contains foul language or religious references is automatically deleted by our anti-spam software and will not be seen. All other communications are welcome.

DISCLAIMER

Please don't be stupid and kill yourself. This book is a work of FICTION. Do not try any new sexual practice that you find in this book. It is fiction and not to be confused with reality. Neither the author nor the publisher or its associates assume any responsibility for any loss, injury, death or legal consequences resulting from acting on the contents in this book. Every character in this book is over 18 years of age. The author's opinions are not to be construed as the opinions of the publisher. The material in this book is for entertainment purposes ONLY. Enjoy.

Erotica Short Stories, Vol. 27

Deepest and Darkest

10 Secret Desire Stories in 1

By: Just Plain Bob

© **Just Plain Bob 2015**
ISBN: 978-1-68030-402-2

Sammi

She had the tightest ass I'd ever slid my cock into and she loved anal sex. She had a cute but sexy squeal as she took it up the dirt road and she had a way of making me feel like no other man in the world could fuck her ass as good as I could.

Her mouth was like a vacuum cleaner and her blow jobs were state of the art, but it was her cunt that damned near enslaved me. It felt like hot crushed velvet and she could make her muscles make you think that there was a hand inside her pussy jacking you off while you thought you were fucking her.

She had the face of an angel, the body of a sex goddess. There was only one thing wrong with her – she was another man's wife.

I remember the night I met Sammi. I had just returned home from spending three years as a member of Uncle Sam's Green Machine. That afternoon I'd taken my car out of storage and had gone to NAPA to get the parts I needed for a tune-up. The guy behind the counter was Charlie Biggens, a guy I had gone through high school with. We shot the bull for a bit and before I left with my parts, we had made arrangements to meet that night at the Smokehouse, a bar on the outskirts of town.

When I got there, I found that Charlie had rounded up several of my other old high school buds. We were sitting at the table sipping beer and catching up when there was a sudden hush, and all eyes seemed to look to the front door. I looked that way and what I saw took my breath away. Tall, maybe 5'9" and absolutely drop dead gorgeous. Long red hair, green eyes and a body to die for.

The hush had been momentary, not much more than a fraction of a second but still noticeable, and then the noise level resumed. The woman looked around the room and I heard Charlie say, almost under his breath, "Not here damn it, not here."

It was almost as if she had heard him because her head turned to our direction and her eyes locked on to our table. She smiled and headed our way and Charlie muttered, "Oh fuck me."

The woman walked up to our table, pulled out a chair and sat down. She looked around the table and then in a low sultry voice said, "Which one of you studs wants to buy a lady a drink?"

Charlie waived the waitress over and the woman ordered Tequila with salt and lime. Then she looked around the table and her sparkling eyes settled on me.

"Charlie, introduce me to your friend."

"Sammi, this is Harry; Harry, meet Sammi."

"That's Sammi with an eye sweetie, not a wye."

Her gaze was cool and appraising and as I shook her hand, I swear that touching her made me tingle all the way down to my toes. Her drink arrived and as she put the salt on her left hand, I saw the wedding rings – and all the thoughts I'd been having evaporated.

Sammi sat, drank and listened to the conversation as Charlie, Frank, Bud and Bill asked me about Kuwait, Afghanistan and Iraq and what had it been like to be in the Army. I asked them what they had been up to while I'd been gone and while the conversation went on, a band had come in and set up. As soon as they started playing, Sammi stood up and said, "Come on Charlie, dance with me."

I could see the reluctance on his face, but he got up and moved out onto the dance floor with her. "What's her story?" I asked when she and Charlie were away from the table. "Married woman in a bar at a table with a bunch of guys?"

"Her old man works swing shift and she doesn't like to sit at home and stare at the walls. She comes in, drinks and dances, and then he stops by and picks her up on the way home."

"Charlie didn't seem all that eager to dance with her."

"She used to be Charlie's girl before she got married."

"He let something like that get away? Was he on drugs?"

I saw all the guys glance at each other and then Frank said, "You would have to ask Charlie about that."

Over the next hour or so, Sammi had danced with all of the guys at our table except me, and that was because I hadn't asked her. The fact that I wasn't in any hurry to get her out on the dance floor must have bugged her so she got up and came over to me. She took my arm and said, "Come on sweetie, your turn."

Once on the floor, I tried to hold her away, but she moved in close – real close – and I tried to pull back. "Don't panic sweetie, I'm not going to rape you, I just like to be close. I can follow your lead better if I can feel how your body is moving."

She cocked her head to one side and I felt those cool green eyes boring into me. "Are you gay sweetie?"

"No."

"Just wondering. Most men fall all over themselves trying to get me to dance with them, but I got the definite impression that if I hadn't come to you, you weren't going to come to me."

"You read me right."

"Might a poor girl ask why?"

"You are married and I've learned from bitter experience not to have anything to do with a married woman. Even something as innocent as a dance can get a jealous husband fired up."

"You do know what an attitude like that can get you, don't you?"

"No."

"My interest, sweetie. I like a challenge."

"Is that your way of saying that you fuck around on your husband?"

"You are blunt, aren't you?"

"Just don't believe in wasting a whole lot of time."

"To answer your question, I haven't yet, but I've not said no to the possibility. You never know about those things. All it takes is for the right man to come along."

"Well, I'm not him. I don't mess around with another man's woman."

"Oh shuckey darn. I was so looking forward to having you chase me and try to get me onto your back seat. You have destroyed my dreams. Oh cruel fate. So tell me, is that a roll of quarters pressing into my leg?"

Right then the music ended and I walked her back to the table. True to her word, I had gotten her interest: when she wasn't dancing with whomever asked, she was trying to talk to me. But as desirable as she was, I couldn't get past the rings on her fingers. I finally got so uncomfortable with her attention that I got up, made my excuses and left.

***

I got a call from Charlie the next day.

"What did you say to Sammi last night?"

"Nothing. She got pissed because I didn't ask her to dance and then didn't seem to like it when I told her that I didn't have anything to do with married women. Why?"

"After you left she pumped everyone at the table for information about you."

We arranged to meet for a beer that evening and he started right out by warning me about Sammi.

"She's no good Harry. She looks like an angel, but she's rotten to the core. Don't let her get her hooks into you."

"No fear old buddy, I meant it when I said that I don't have anything to do with married women. I heard that she was your girl before she got married. She must have fucked over you pretty bad for you to feel that way about her."

"It wasn't what she did to me; it was what she tried to do to me."

"What was that?"

"Her big turn on is to have guys fight over her. That's how I ended up with her in the first place."

"How's that?"

"She came in here one night with a guy and about an hour later, he came over to me and told me that his girl didn't like the way I was looking at her. I told him that I hadn't been looking at her at all, let alone in any particular way, but if it would make her feel better I would move so that I would be looking in the opposite direction. I got up, moved my chair and sat back down with my back to her. He went back to their table and she said something to him. Then he got up and left her sitting there and never came back.

"Maybe an hour later, she got up and came over to me, told me that she had a problem and that it was all my fault. She told me that whatever I had said to her boyfriend had scared him so bad that he had taken off and that she didn't have a ride home. I said no problem, gave her a ride home and she asked me to give her a call. I called and we started dating. After we had been going together for about two months, she felt that she had me wrapped around her finger – she was great pussy Harry, the best ever – and she thought that I would do anything to keep her.

"One night we were at Hank's Bar and Grill and she told me that she doesn't like the way this guy was looking at her. She said he kept smiling at her and licking his lips. I got up and went over to his table and he said, "Bug off fuck face." I dragged him outside and stomped the shit out of him. Sammi was insatiable that night and for the next week she couldn't keep her hands off me. Two weeks later it happened again. Same results and she tried to destroy me sexually.

"Three weeks later it happened again and only by that time had I figured it out. The two times with me and the night I had supposedly run off her boyfriend showed a pattern. Anyway, I told her, if she didn't like being looked at, to start wearing a sack dress, stuff her hair under a hat and stop wearing makeup. Then I got the "What kind of a man are you that you'll let another man do something like that to me" speech. I told her that I was the kind of man who wasn't stupid, that I knew what she was doing and I wasn't going to play that game.

"That ended it for us. She went through four more boyfriends and a dozen fights before she met the guy she married. He likes to fight and all she has to do is point him in the direction she wants him to go. She has changed her game a bit in the last year. Now she comes in here, comes onto a guy, gets him out into the parking lot to neck; waits for hubby to come in, see what's going on and go into a jealous rage and then the fight is on.

"She's evil Harry. A great looker and a fantastic piece of ass, but pure fucking evil. And from what I saw last night, she has set her sights on you."

"I told you Charlie, I don't have anything to do with married women."

"Best keep it that way Harry. Best thing would be to find another bar to have your drinks at.

***

Two days later, I was at the Smokehouse sitting at the bar and drinking beer when Sammi came in. She looked around, saw me, and then came over and took the stool next to me.

"Hey sailor, buy a thirsty girl a drink?"

I waved the barmaid over and Sammi ordered Tequila. The band was just starting to play and she said, "Come on Harry, dance with me."

"No thanks."

"Oh that's right, I forgot. You are afraid of married women."

"Not afraid, I just don't need the trouble they bring."

"What possible kind of trouble could come out of you dancing with me?"

"A jealous husband coming in and seeing us together, comes to mind."

"Oh come on. Fred doesn't get off work for another three hours. The soonest he can be here is eleven forty-five, so you can dance with me until eleven-forty and then go and hide."

"Sammi, just go away and play your sick little games with someone else."

She gave me a nasty look, got off the barstool and stormed away. The barmaid came over to me and said, "You are kind of cute, but I'm curious, are you gay?"

"That's the second time someone has asked me that in this bar."

"Just naturally curious, honey. I've never seen any man turn her down and I've never, ever seen her get up and storm away from a man like she just did."

"No secret. I don't mess with another man's woman and she's married. If I didn't already know that and she hadn't had her rings on, I'd have been after her in a flash."

"Oh my, a man with principles. Girls like that in a guy."

"They do?"

"Most definitely honey."

"Well then, I guess that brings up the question, do you like a man with principles?"

"Yes I do."

"Maybe we could get together and talk about it."

"Maybe we could."

"What time do you get off work?"

"My shift ends in an hour, but I'm telling you ahead of time that all you are going to get is talk."

"A man has to start somewhere. I'm Harry."

"Hi Harry, I'm Lisa."

When Lisa and I left together, I happened to look Sammi's way and the look she gave me was not at all nice.

***

Lisa and I started dating and I got in the habit of stopping by the Smokehouse just before the end of her shift and then we would leave together. It was a Saturday night and when I walked in I saw Charlie and Frank sitting at a table, so I joined them. I hadn't been there ten minutes when Sammi came in with some mean looking dude. His nose was bent from where it had been broken a couple of times and he had some scars around his eyes. I looked at Charlie, "The husband?"

"Yeah, that's him."

Half an hour went by and then I saw Sammi and her husband looking my way. A minute later, he got up and headed for our table. He stood there, looked right at me and said, "Hey asshole, my wife don't ..." but he never got to finish what he was going to say because my hand shot up, grabbed the front of his shirt and I jerked him down until his face smashed onto the table. I stood up, grabbed the hair on the back of his head and slammed him face first onto the table twice more. Still holding his hair, I grabbed the back of his belt and dragged him outside into the parking lot.

A small crowd followed us out and I asked, "Which car is his?" It was pointed out to me and I dragged him over to it, slammed his face into the hood a couple of times and then let him fall in a heap on the ground. I looked around at the crowd to see if anyone was upset enough to come help him; but with one exception, all I saw were people who had looks on their faces that seemed to say, "About time."

The one exception was Sammi. Her eyes were bright and feverish and she looked like she'd just had an orgasm. It pissed me off. Because of her and her 'jones,' her husband had suffered, all the men she had sicced her husband on had suffered, and before her husband, god alone only knew how many men had paid a price just so she could get her jollies. On an impulse I walked over to where she was standing.

"Satisfied now? Did you get what you wanted out of this?"

It was like my words snapped her out of a trance and she looked at me with confusion on her face and said, "What?"

"I said are you happy now? Did you get off on seeing it?"

"I have no idea of what you are talking about."

When she said that, it pissed me off even more. I looked around at the crowd and then said, "Most of you know where I live. When he gets up off the ground, tell him that if he wants his wife, he'll have to come to my place to get her."

I grabbed her by the wrist and pulled her over to my car. I opened the driver's side door, pushed her inside and then I followed her. I started the car, pulled out of the lot and turned for home. Sammi was leaning against the door on the passenger side and she said, "Where are you taking me?"

"To my place."

"Why? Why are you doing this to me?"

"It is what you wanted, isn't it? Men fighting over you? Well the fight is over sweetie and to the victor goes the spoils. You are now mine by right of conquest. Doesn't that just make your loins tingle?"

"Stop the car. Stop the car right now and let me out."

"Can't do that sweetie. You heard me tell everyone that I was taking you to my place and to tell your hubby that he had to go there to get you, so you have to be there when he comes. Meanwhile, we need to put our time together to good use."

I unzipped my pants, pulled out my cock and then said, "Get over here and suck it."

She stared at it for almost a minute, and just as I began to think she was going to tell me to go to hell, she moved across the seat toward me and lowered her head into my lap. I hadn't expected her to do that. I was just fucking with her and trying to humiliate her, but when her mouth surrounded me, I stopped thinking about anything except getting off in her mouth. I pulled over and parked and let her work her magic, and I do have to say that it was the best head I had ever received. I didn't tell her when I was ready to shoot, but when I did, she didn't jerk her head back; she just clamped her lips tight on me and swallowed what I spit out.

When she was done and my cock was nothing but a limp noodle, she sat up and said, "Satisfied?"

"Yes and no."

"What does that mean?"

"It means that I am satisfied right now, but that by the time we get to my place I won't be. My plan had been to just take you home with me and wait for your husband to humiliate himself by having to come and ask me for you, but after that superb blow job I've decided to let you try and fuck my brains out."

"And you think I will?"

"Why not? You just sucked my cock without being forced."

For the rest of the ride to my place she just leaned against the door and looked at me with those cool, green appraising eyes.

***

Once in my apartment, I showed her the bedroom and she asked, "And just what are you expecting?"

"Nothing. I didn't expect the blow job. Thank you by the way, it was great."

"If you don't expect anything, why am I here?"

"I just thought that it was time that you found out that there are consequences when you fuck with other people. I think that it will do a lot of people good to see your husband have to come here and ask me to give you back. And, it might make you think twice before playing your little game again."

"So what are you going to do to me?"

"Whatever you want."

"What I want?"

"Yes Sammi, whatever you want. I don't believe in rape. You are free to walk out that door anytime you want. You could have gotten out of the car at any one of the stop lights or stop signs we hit on the way home. In fact, I'm surprised that you didn't. I guess you came along because you expect to see us get into it again when he shows up to get you, right?"

"No, not at all right. I didn't get out because I don't dare go back home now."

"I don't follow."

"You took me by surprise when you hustled me into your car. I didn't get my shit together until after we were out of the parking lot. When I told you to stop and let me out and you didn't and kept on driving, that pretty much sealed my fate."

"How's that?"

"If you had stopped, I could have walked back and Fred would have seen that not enough time had passed for anything to have happened. By keeping on going, you stretched out the interval and now nothing I say will make him believe that nothing happened. He will be sure in his own mind that you had me and he will never believe that I didn't let you do it willingly. If I walk out of here now and go home, he will hurt me. I'm afraid that you just got yourself a permanent house guest."

"Permanent?"

"At least until Fred leaves town."

"Nonsense. He'll be here to get you by dinner time."

"No he won't, sweetie. As far as he's concerned, I'm damaged goods now and his pride will never let him take me back except to punish me – and he won't waste his time coming for me to do just that."

She walked into the bedroom and started undressing.

"What are you doing?"

"When you told God and everyone you were bringing me here, you gave me the name sweetie; and as long as I have the name, I may as well play the game."

***

That was six months ago and so far she has been proven right.

Fred didn't come for her and after two weeks, she went to her place (while Fred was at work) and got all of her stuff and moved in with me. Not exactly what I wanted; but hey, I caused it. I made it happen. I've taken her to the Smokehouse a couple of times on weekends. The first time, Fred was there and he left as soon as he saw us come in. The next time we were already there and he turned and left as soon as he saw us.

So far she hasn't pulled the "I don't like the way he is looking at me" shit on me, but maybe that's because I told her that as far as I was concerned, she wasn't worth fighting over.

"You pull that shit on me and I'll just get up and walk away from you, go home and throw all your shit out on the front lawn."

Sammi hasn't seen a lawyer yet and, as far as I know, neither has Fred. So even though she is living with me, she is still married to him.

***

The down side of Sammi living with me is what it did to my relationship with Lisa. Two days after my altercation with Fred, Lisa called me.

"Are you okay?"

"Yeah, I'm all right."

"When her husband got up off the ground, he stomped around telling everyone he was going to kill you. Watch out for him."

"I will."

"Did you do her when you got to your place?"

"I hadn't intended to, but yeah, I did. It seemed like one more way I could rub his nose in it."

"Well you made a lot of people happy by doing what you did, and I don't blame you because they have both had it coming for a long time. Is she still there?"

"Yes. Fred hasn't come to get her and she says she is afraid to leave and go home to him."

"As I remember it, you only have the one bed and no couch."

"Yes, that's right."

"To me that means you are sharing the bed. If that's the case and you already did her when you got her to your place... I'm betting that you are still doing her. Am I right?"

As I looked down at Sammi working on my cock with her mouth, I knew that there wasn't anything I could say, and my silence spoke for itself.

"I thought so," Lisa said. "I've always wanted to be able to play a couple of musical instruments Harry, but second fiddle isn't one of them. Give me a call when you get rid of her and maybe, if I'm not taken, we can do something."

I put the phone down and Sammi took her mouth off me long enough to ask, "Who was it sweetie?"

"A missed opportunity, honey. Just keep sucking."

End of the 1st Story

Sell, Baby, Sell

It was enough to make me want to scream! I worked my butt off for six weeks to land the deal and then the asshole – who was supposed to be working with me but didn't do a damn thing, except ask me once a week how things were going – got half the commission and a promotion. Don't ever let people tell you that women in the work place are not discriminated against – I'm living proof that they don't have a clue what they are talking about.

I've worked for the XYZ Corporation for eleven years now; and even though for eight of those eleven years I have been the highest grossing salesperson in the corporation, I have never received a promotion.Raises, yes; bonuses, yes; but promotions, no! I've watched as one incompetent after another move up the corporate ladder with absolutely nothing going for them, except that they play golf and play cards with the right people. But for a woman, even playing golf or cards with the right people isn't enough. I played poker once with the guys in upper management and was never asked to play again. I guess I hurt the VP's feelings when I bluffed him out of a fair sized pot. I've also played golf, once anyway, with the boys from upper management. The men's tee boxes on the course were being readied for a tournament and we all had to play from the woman's tees. Should have been an advantage for the boys, right? I beat them all by four strokes and was never asked to play with them again. Ron – the clown I had to share my commission with – beat them by seven strokes when he played with them, got a pat on the back for being a good golfer and was invited back. I beat them and we have to sweep it under the table because it would look bad if it got out they were beat by a girl.

My husband tells me that I'm paranoid and that XYZ doesn't have anything against women moving up. "All companies are the same sweetie. They all want what's best for the bottom line. If you aren't being picked, it is because they don't think you have what it takes. Being a good ole boy has nothing to do with who gets promotions in modern day business."

"Bullshit! What about the time the regional sales manager's job was open and they told me that Hawkins and I were the only ones being considered, and they told us both that whoever performed the best would get the job? I outsold Hawkins three to one and brought in nine new accounts to his three and they still gave that lame ass the promotion."

"He must have had some quality that they felt they needed; some quality that you couldn't offer."

My husband is the perfect case in point. I love him dearly, but that doesn't make me blind where he is concerned. He is the prototypical good ole boy. He takes his clients on golfing weekends to Hilton Head. He hosts poker games and he takes them sports fishing on the Gulf. He lands lots of business for his company, which leads to more poker, golf and fishing. As a result he has been promoted twice in the last eighteen months. Yet I have more sales and managerial ability in one of my pussy hairs than he has in his entire body and still I get constantly passed over.

The thing with Ron was the last straw. I had finally had enough and I sat down and composed my letter of resignation. My husband convinced me to sit on it for a couple of weeks, a cool down period of sorts, and I agreed. Nine days later, there were some changes in upper management and all of a sudden I had a new vice president to report to. I put my resignation on hold until I could see how things would shake out.

A week after Chad took over as VP, he called me into his office and asked me if I could attend a conference with him in New York.

"It is an industry thing, but I expect that there might be some opportunities for us there. You seem to be my top grosser and I'd like to have you along."

Was I going to say no? This was the first time at XYZ that

anyone at his level had even acknowledged that I was something other than just another girl on the payroll. Of course I would go.

As far as industry conferences went, there were no surprises. A lot of talk on common problems, some boring talks by executives full of themselves and a general round of information sharing. The real business got taken care of at the dinner and cocktail party following the day's conference. After dinner I circulated and renewed friendships, talked with people I had done business with in the past, and made a few contacts that would be worth following up on. I was on my fifth margarita and being thankful that I didn't have to drive home that night when Chad came over and sat down with me.

"This is the first chance I've had to sit down with you and chat."

I took a sip of my margarita and said, "Feel free to chat away."

"I understand that you are dissatisfied with the way you feel that the company has been treating you."

"I guess that is a pretty fair statement of the facts. Enough so that my letter of resignation has already been written."

"Has anyone ever taken the time to explain why you keep getting passed over?"

"No, but even if they had, it wouldn't change that fact that they keep selecting incompetents and then, to add insult to injury, they place me under those incompetents."

"Is it just a title thing with you?"

"What do you mean?"

"Is it just a title you are after?"

"No, I really believe that I can do a better job than the clowns they keep picking."

"Maybe you could, but does the job need, as you put it, to be done better?"

"I'm not following you."

"Does the paper need to be shuffled any better? Is there a crying need for the weekly sales meeting to be held any better? What I'm getting at is that you are the top grosser in the company and what you do does more for the company's bottom line than anything you could do if you got moved up. You might be a better paper pusher than the guys that moved up, but if you had moved up sales would have gone down. Not only that, but the people who would have had to take your place could have cost us some of the business that you had already brought in. Right now you are making more in commissions than the guys who got promoted are making in salary."

"That's not true and you know it. When you add the perks that go with the promotions they are way ahead of me. They get a company car and a company gas credit card. I have to buy my own car and pay for my own gas. They get larger expense accounts with wider latitude on what they can claim as a business expense. They get stock options, better health and dental, special retirement plans and so on. Plus not constantly being on the road during the week, better vacation time, bonuses at the end of the year based on how well their division, meaning me, does in sales. Add all that up and they damn sure are not making less than I am."

Chad sat quietly looking at me and then he said, "How bad do you want all those things that you just mentioned?"

"What are you getting at?"

"Simple question, how bad?"

"Everybody wants to make a good living Chad, and everybody

wants their worth recognized. I'm no different."

"Okay then, what if you could get all the perks that you just mentioned and you stayed where you are, doing what you do better than anyone else in the company. How bad would you want something like that? What would you be willing to do?"

I had a feeling that I knew where this was headed, but I planned on making him be much more specific before I threw my drink in his face. "Let us assume that I don't know what you are getting at and go right to what you would expect me to do."

He smiled at me. "Whoa there honey, you got me all wrong, well maybe only partially. What I have in mind is creating a position that will satisfy the policy and procedures manual and allow me to give you the perks you want, and still leave you able to sell and bring in new business. We will call it something like Special Assistant to the Vice President of Sales. You just have to decide just how bad you want the position. I'm going to give you a situation and then I'm going to get up and leave you to think about it. Okay so far?"

"Go ahead, I'm listening."

"See that tall man over there by the punch bowl? That is Jason Royal. I've been trying to get his business for ten years now. His account would be worth 3.5 to 5 million a year for the company. Tonight I asked him straight out what I had to do to get his business. He smiled at me and pointed at you. "Make her my account representative. If she services the account, and I do mean *services*, you have a deal." Let me be totally clear here. Your job does not depend on what you decide. The only question on the table is how bad do you want the perks of the new position I will create for you, let alone the commissions that the account will generate."

He got up to leave, but then he turned back to me, "One more thing that I need to be clear on. I wouldn't mind a taste of you myself, but that has to be a matter of your choice and outside of the work place," and he walked away leaving me staring at his back.

There was absolutely no way that I would even remotely consider what Chad was suggesting – none at all – and yet two margaritas later, I found myself dancing with Mr. Royal. He had approached me and had asked me to dance and I accepted. He was a perfect gentleman and never gave me any indication that he had spoken to Chad about me. We danced two numbers and then he asked me to join him at his table and I did. As I worked my way through another margarita, we sat and talked and I found him to be very charming and witty. As the party wound down and people were leaving, he told me that he had enjoyed my company and that he hoped he would see me again someday. I don't know which of us was the most surprised when I said, "Why? The night isn't over yet."

I was an absolute slut. I did things with Jason that I had never done with anyone else, not even with my husband. Jason gave me a rim job and I had my first ever anal sex and I loved it. Then I gave him a rim job and followed it up with the best head I was able to give. We used each other for sexual release – no tenderness, no pretense of affection – just plain old down and dirty sex. He fucked me hard and I screamed at him to fuck me harder, to make me his bitch and to cum in me. The last thing I remember before falling asleep was Jason calling the front desk for a six-thirty wake up-call and ordering breakfast for two from room service.

The telephone rang at six twenty-nine and before Jason hung up I had his cock in my mouth; and as soon as he was hard I mounted him and bounced up and down on his cock until room service knocked on the door. As soon as the door closed behind the waiter, Jason pushed me down on the bed and we were half an hour late for the first meeting of the morning.

Jason and I sat next to each other at lunch and I played with his cock under the table. We went right to my room after the afternoon's last conference and never did make it to that evening's cocktail party. The night was a repeat of the previous evening, except for two things – it lasted longer and it got a little kinky.

Jason was on the toilet and I was using the break in the action to call home. I was talking to my husband when Jason came out of the bathroom. He started fingering my pussy and I was holding the phone in one hand while trying to fend him off with the other. He grinned at me, pushed me around until he was behind me and then he took me from behind while I was telling my hubby that it was just another boring conference and that I couldn't wait to get home to him.

The funny thing was I wasn't lying. I did want to hurry home to him. I loved the big old bear and I would find some way to make it up to him for what I was doing behind his back. Jason and I didn't leave a wakeup call for in the morning – we never went to sleep.

The conference broke at noon the next day and Jason asked me to stop by his room when we went up to get our bags. As soon as the door closed behind us he pulled me over to the bed, bent me forward at the waist so I had to support myself with my hands on the bed and then he entered me from behind and fucked me one last time.

When it was over and I had come out of the bathroom after cleaning myself up, he handed me an envelope. "What' this?"

"The contract. Signed, sealed and delivered."

"Oh no you don't," I said as I handed the envelope back to him. "I did what I did because I wanted to, not to get your business. In fact, I'll be extremely disappointed if you don't try to see me again."

"You mean that?"

"Absolutely."

We were alone in the elevator on the way down to the lobby and just before the door opened I reached over and gave his cock a squeeze, "Don't forget me baby," and then I walked over to wait for the courtesy car to the airport.

I was sitting next to Chad on the flight home. I had been staring out the window wondering how I could love my husband as much as I did and still want to be Jason's slut. I didn't love Jason as a person, although I did like him, but I loved fucking him and I wanted to do it again.

In the window glass I noticed Chad looking over at me. I turned to him and said, "What?"

"Oh nothing."

"It must be something for you to look at me like that."

"I guess I'm just jealous."

"Jealous of what?"

"The smile that has been on Jason Royal's face for the last two days."

I think I might have even blushed.

"By the way, what kind of car do you want?"

"What do you mean what kind of car?"

"Your new company car Ms. Special Assistant. When Jason handed me the contract he told me to make sure that I did whatever I had to do keep his account rep happy. He thinks you are pretty special."

I smiled at that. "He isn't all that bad either."

"There you go making me jealous again."

I looked over at Chad and the events of the last two nights

passed through my mind. What the hell – why not – I was already a slut for my company.

"There's a hotel at the airport, right?"

End of the 2nd Story

Rob's Wedding

The music started and all the guests stood and looked toward the back of the church as the bride, on the arm of her father, started down the aisle toward my son, who stood there watching her walk toward him. Forty-eight hours ago I'd have given odds of ten thousand to one that the wedding would never happen. I still didn't understand why it was taking place, but who in the hell can understand kids these days. Oh well, it was Rob's life to live, not mine, but I would have thought that the night of his bachelor party would have been a wakeup call.

***

"Richard, I'm leaving," my wife hollered up the stairs at me. I walked down the steps and offered her my mouth for a goodbye kiss. She kissed me, slipped me a little tongue and then said:

"Don't wait up for me honey. If this thing goes like most of them, I'll be too blitzed to drive and I'll crash at Melanie's."

"I guess there is something to be said for having the bridal shower at your sister's."

"Do you know what you are going to do yet?"

"Rob and I have decided that it will for sure get drunk out at the bachelor party and we are going to cab home when it is over."

"Well sweetie, if it is your typical bachelor party and they bring in a stripper, you better keep your hands to yourself old man. I want all you got so don't be going and giving my stuff to some young twat who won't appreciate it as much as I will."

She leaned forward, kissed me again, and then left. As I watched her go, I just hoped that Rob would luck out and that Karen would be a wife half as good to him as his mother had been to me.

***

It was your typical bachelor party. Two tables of poker players puffing on cigars and drinking booze and everybody listening with one ear for the knock on the door that would announce the entertainment had arrived. I felt totally out of place. Everyone was Rob's age and I was the only old fogey in attendance. I had known it would be like that and I had tried to get out of coming, but Rob had insisted.

Financially it was a good move on my part because those young guys didn't know how to play poker and I was cleaning up. They were doing all kinds of stupid stuff like holding a pair of fours with an ace kicker and only drawing two cards; or trying to draw to an inside straight. One of them in a hand of seven card stud stayed in until the last card with nothing but an ace, king in the hole against two pair visible on the table. It was like taking candy from a baby. Then they started getting silly with adding wild cards. When Rob's best friend had the deal and called seven card stud with "deuces and jacks and kings with an axe" wild, I gave up playing and went over and sat on the couch and watched the porno tape that someone had brought.

By eleven everybody was antsy because the stripper was a no show, so Jim said, "Let's take the party to the Kit Kat Klub" (which was a topless joint on the other side of town.) I was all for going home myself, but I had promised to ride herd on Rob and keep him from getting in too much trouble so I found myself going along with the rest of them.

I have no idea how we managed to get tables right up front that late at night, but we did and it probably wasn't a good thing for Rob. Karen, the bride to be, was drop dead gorgeous, but she had been short changed when it came to the breast department; and here he was with a front row seat where he could feast his eyes on some of the biggest, firmest and best ta-ta's in the state. The poor guy had to sit there and drool in his beer. What's more, everybody in our party knew it. Since it was Rob's bachelor party, the guys started buying him lap dances. Jim went so far as to tell one of the girls about Rob's status and the size of his intended's chest, and the girls teased him unmercifully when they gave him his lap dances.

By the time the first girl had finished her lap dance, Rob was a quivering wreck. When she walked away leaving Rob with a tent pole in his pants, I knew he was going to end the night with a raging case of blue balls. With the rest of the guys egging the girls on, each lap dance got a little more intense. As it got later and the place started clearing out, it got even better – or worse – depending on how you looked at it. In our city, there are laws regulating what the girls can do and there are people who enforce those laws. Those people go to places like the Kit Kat, pretend to be customers, and try to catch the girls breaking those laws. As the Kit Kat emptied out, leaving only customers that the girls knew were not cops, they got a little raunchier. Bare tits were rubbed on Rob's face, pressed into his chest as the girl sat down and ground herself down on his hard pants-covered cock. One girl even reached down and rubbed it a couple of times with her hand.

Everyone got into the spirit of the thing and Rob and I ended up smashed. Smashed and broke, although we didn't realize how broke until after everyone else had taken off. We were standing in front of the Kit Kat digging through our pockets trying to come up with enough to pay for a cab; once we realized how broke we were, we decided not to bother hailing one. Cabs in our town were notorious for not taking checks, but I did have a credit card and six blocks down the street was the Shangri-La Motel. We walked (actually, we staggered) the six blocks and got a room for the night. It was the last vacancy they had and we were lucky to get it, but then again maybe we weren't all that lucky. The Shangri-La was an old motel: built on the cheap before building codes came around and the walls might as well have been tissue paper.

The room to the south of us had someone who snored louder than a buzz saw for twenty minutes or so and then he would wake up.

The snore would be replaced by a hacking cough until he fell back asleep and then the snore would be back. The room that backed up to us to the east had a drunken couple whose idea of a good time was to fight with each other; and we had to listen as they shouted, screamed and yelled at each other.

But it was the room to the north side of us that was driving me crazy. From what I could tell, hearing the voices coming through the wall, there were two women and five men and they were having what seemed like an orgy. With all the racket, sleep was impossible and we were more or less forced to listen to the sound track of a porn film we couldn't see. They voices were a little distorted by the wall, but what was going on was clear enough:

Woman (1): Oh god, oh god, oh god that's good. Push deep, push it in, push it deep. Harder, oh god please give it to me harder.

Man (1): Jesus she is tight.

Man (2): You think she's tight wait until you try this one's ass. I don't think that it has seen cock in quite a while.

Woman (2): Umph, oohg, aahhh.

Man (3): Shouldn't try to talk with your mouth full honey.

Woman (2): Mupth en blrlhpt.

In the background behind that little exchange, Woman (1) was constantly moaning out, "Oh god, oh god, oh god yes, harder, fuck me harder."

Man (3): Hurry up man, you've been in her ass forever. I want a chance to fuck her.

Man (4): I'm tired of waiting. Open your mouth honey.

Woman (1): I don't do that for anyone but my husband.

Man (4): You do tonight sweetie.

Woman (1): I said I don't.....mphglorp umph.

Man (4): That's a girl, suck it sweetie, suck it.

Man (5): Come on you guys, I've been waiting almost ten minutes now.

Man (1): I'm almost ready to blow. Get on over here and get ready; we need to keep this hot bitch going.

Man (4): Keep her going? Shit man, the problem with this one is going to be staying with her. Either her hubby doesn't take care of business or she comes out to play to keep from fucking him into an early grave.

Man (5): Let's do a three holer on one of them.

Man (4): Which one?

Man (5): The young one. She already has a cock in her mouth and in her ass.

Man (1): No can do guys. She said ass and mouth only. Pussy belongs to her boyfriend and you all agreed before we left the bar.

Man (5): Okay, the married one then.

Man (1): I'm gonna cum sweetie, get ready.

Woman (1): *A rather loud and insistent,* "Umph ooogh."

Man (1): What? Take your cock out of her mouth Joe, I can't understand what she's saying.

Woman (2): Not in me damn it, you promised me you wouldn't cum in me.

Man (5): Jesus Ralph, did you have to blow all over her stomach?

Man (1): It had to go somewhere.

Man (5): Christ what a mess. Let me get a towel and clean her off.

Man (4): I'm next in her cunt.

Man (3): I get her ass. Looks like you get her mouth Tom.

Woman (1): Now wait a minute here. I've never done that. I've never had more than two before.

Man (4): You will love it sweetie.

Woman (1): What do I do?

Man (4): I lay down on my back and you sit on my dick and then you lean forward and Sam will slide his cock in your ass. As soon as you get comfortable Tom will take your mouth.

Woman (1): I don't like oral. The taste of cum makes me sick to my stomach.

Man (4): Okay. Hear that guys? No cumming in her mouth.

Woman (1): You have to go slow and easy on my butt. I don't do much anal because my husband is too big.

Man (4): Herb told me that you love taking cock in your ass.

Woman (1): I do, but I can't let my husband because of his size. The only time I can do it is when I'm out partying and even then if the guy I end up with is too big I won't let him.

Man (3): How about it, mine, okay?

Woman (1): Oh yes, that's a nice one.

Man (2): Who is next on little cupcake here? I'm ready to blow in her ass and from the way she is pushing back at me she doesn't want to stop.

Man (5): Me, I'm up next.

Woman (2): I'm cumming. Oh god I'm cumming.

***

It went on that way for hours as the men took turns on the two women. Two and three at a time on woman (1) and two at a time on woman (2). I could see the effect that it was having on Rob. He still had blue balls from the Kit Kat Klub and what was going on next door to us had him squirming. He didn't want to whip it out and stroke off with me there, but he needed relief. I laughed and pointed at the wall:

"Why don't you go and knock on their door? You can tell them that their noise is keeping you awake and since you are up anyway maybe you can join them."

I meant it as a joke, but I could see that he was giving it some serious thought. Not that I blamed him. I liked anal sex and there did seem to be a lot of that going on next door. I also wondered at the contrast between the two women. One was referred to as older and married and the other was called the 'young one'. Oh well, wishful thinking on my part. In twenty-three years of marriage I had never been unfaithful to my wife. Never had any need to. While other guys bitched and moaned about only getting sex from their wives once or twice a week, Fran was still pulling me into the bedroom four and five times a week.

It was getting light out and I checked my watch and saw that it was almost six. The Safeway across from the Kit Kat would open at six and I could get a check cashed and we could get a cab and go home. Next door I heard woman (1) say:

"No more guys. You have to get me back to my car and I need to get home to my hubby."

"You going to give him sloppy seconds?"

"Good lord no. Hopefully I'll get home just in time to kiss him goodbye before he leaves for work. I'll be all clean and sweet smelling for him when he gets home tonight."

"Can we do this again?"

"I don't see why not, but you can't call me so give me a number where I can reach you."

"Both of you?"

"I can only speak for myself."

"How about it cupcake? You want to do it again?"

Woman (2) replied, "I had fun. Yeah, I think I would like to do it again, but it may be a while before I can. I'm going to be real busy for the next two or three weeks."

I looked at my watch and said, "Come on Rob, let's get out of here." We stepped out into the light of the rising sun just as the door to the room next door opened, and two giggling women walked out followed by five guys.

I heard a sharp "Oh God" and I turned to see Fran and Karen standing there. Rob saw Karen – his face turned pale and he threw up on the sidewalk.

***

I have no idea what transpired between Rob and Karen in the forty-eight hours following that scene, but there she was, coming down the aisle toward him. I don't know where Fran was; I'm sure that she was somewhere in the church in the rows behind me, but I didn't care enough to look. I had tossed her ass out of the house and then had called a divorce lawyer and made an appointment for the coming Tuesday.

I promised myself I would be civil toward her and smile when the photographer took the family part of the wedding pictures; if there indeed were any pictures taken. I was still flirting with the idea of standing up and saying a few choice words when the minister goes the part about:

"Is there anyone present who knows of a reason why this union should not take place? Let them speak now, or forever hold their peace."

I was thinking on it; I was thinking on it hard.

End of the 3rd Story

———⚬✄⚬———

Sally's Birthday

I sat there stunned as my wife moved out onto the dance floor with the man. Had I really heard her right, or had I had too much to drink that it was confusing what the words coming from her actually were?

It was Friday night and Sally's birthday and we were out celebrating. We went to the Landing Strip and settled down for an evening of drinking and dancing. Well, drinking for me; drinking *and* dancing for Sally. A land mine during the First Gulf War had put an end to my tripping the light fantastic; but Sally loved to dance, so I sucked it up, put a lid on my jealous nature and let her dance with who ever asked.

Sally was in a good mood and I had thought that was a good thing since things hadn't been going all that well for us lately. But the bomb she had just laid on me told me that her good mood wasn't good for *me*, not even a little bit. Even if she didn't follow through on what she'd said, the fact that she had said it was not going to go away.

***

The Gulf War had given me another problem besides my bad leg. It had given me some form of erectile dysfunction that the doctors just couldn't seem to nail down. They could find no physical reason for the problem so they were assuming that it was mental, but so far the head doctors hadn't found anything either. From the way they talked, I got the impression that I was the only known case of whatever it was that I had.

The problem was that the condition came and went. I would have hard-ons galore for seven or eight months, and then one morning I would get up and Mr. Happy wouldn't. Blow jobs, porn movies and even the sexy big titted babes at the strip joint couldn't get me up. For two or three months my cock would lie dormant, and then one day I would wake up with 'morning wood' and for the next eight or ten months I would be fine.

This had been going on for the last ten years and I had pretty much adjusted to the fact that every eight months or so, I was going to go 'out of service' for two or three months; and while my wife Sally wasn't happy about it, she too learned to live with it. We managed fine for a little over nine years and then things got bad. The eight months of good times ended and the out of service time began, but this time it lasted longer than two or three months.

It had been fourteen months now since I had last been able to meet Sally's needs. The last eight months had been really bad. Sally was constantly irritable and she found fault with everything I did. She would light into me over some little thing and then the next day she would apologize. Then not an hour later she would be on me for something else. I knew what was wrong; I knew why she was being the way she was and I did my best to ride with it, but I'm only human and every once in a while I would bark back at her, and then things would be really chilly around the house for a while. We were in one of those cold periods when I decided to take Sally out dancing for her birthday.

***

It started out well. We were not strangers at the Landing Strip and quite a few of the regulars knew the circumstances behind my sitting and sipping my drink while Sally danced the night away. So it was no surprise when as soon as we sat down a guy showed up to ask Sally to dance. The first hour went by and things went as they usually did, with Sally being almost constantly on the dance floor, and then things began to change a bit. I noticed that she was dancing most of the dances with the same three guys. And then I began to notice some things that I hadn't noticed till then. Things like how close she was dancing with them, where their hands were and how she was responding. She wasn't doing anything to stop them or slow them down.

The set ended and the band took their break and I waited for Sally to come back to our table so I could ask her what she thought she was doing. But Sally didn't come back to our table – she went and sat at the table with the three guys she had been dancing with. They were soon laughing and talking. I saw one of the men place a hand pretty high up on her leg and she didn't push it away, but she did turn and look at me and smile an evil little smile. After several minutes, she got up and walked over to our table and said:

"I don't think I'll be going home with you tonight."

"What?"

"My friends want to party with me. And since you can't, I've decided to do it."

She turned and walked back to the three men and the band started playing again and she pulled one of them up and moved out onto the dance floor. I sat there watching her and wondered if she'd lost her mind. The song ended and she and the guy went back to the table and sat down. When I saw the man she had just danced with run his hand up under her skirt, I'd had enough. I got up and walked over to the table and told Sally we were leaving and to grab her purse.

"I told you I'm not going home with you. My friends want to party with me, right guys?"

They all smiled and I said, "Okay, your choice." I reached over her shoulder and picked up her purse, opened it and took out her key ring. I dropped the purse in her lap, took the key ring and removed the house key from it, dropped the rest of the keys on top of her purse and walked away from her as she was saying:

"What are you doing? Why did you do that?"

I didn't answer her and I walked out of the bar. I got in the car, started it and waited about five minutes to see if she would come running out. When she didn't, I moved the car across the street, parked in the supermarket parking lot and settled down to watch the bar parking lot.

Maybe five minutes later Sally came out and walked through the lot looking for me; and when she didn't find me, she walked back into the bar. Half an hour later she came out with one of the guys she had been sitting with and they got into a car. I expected to see it start up and pull out of the lot so the man could run Sally home, but nothing happened. I couldn't see into the car from where I was parked so I kept sitting there and watching.

After maybe twenty minutes, the man got out of the car and went back into the bar; minutes later a second man from the table came out and went to the car. Twenty minutes went by and then I saw him go back into the bar and the third man came out. By then I knew what was going on; but as they say, seeing is believing.

I gave him a minute or two and then I got out of the car, walked across the street to the bar parking lot and moved to where I thought I could see what was going on without being noticed. I found a spot behind the car parked next to them where I could see and hear. I heard Sally's voice and I could see she was naked from the waist down. She was bent over the man and was sucking his cock. She slurped on him for a couple of minutes and then they changed positions. She got on her back and spread her legs wide and waited. The man maneuvered between her legs and then worked his cock into her as she cried out:

"That's it, fuck me, fuck your whore, fuck me hard."

I could see his ass rising and falling and hear the 'slap, slap, slap' of flesh meeting flesh. I watched for maybe ten minutes and then he said:

"I'm gonna cum."

"Not in me, not in me, you guys promised that you wouldn't cum in me."

The guy pulled out of her and shot his wad all over her stomach. Sally leaned forward and licked his cock clean.

"Who do you want next?"

"No one baby, at least not tonight. I've got to get cleaned up and then you have to run me home."

"You going to be all right?"

"He'll be pissed, but I can handle him."

"When can we do this again?"

"Give me a call at work and I'll see about taking a long lunch hour. Now come on. I really do need to get home."

***

I went back to my car, drove home and made sure that the house was locked up tight, windows and doors, and then I sat back and waited. About a half-hour went by and a car pulled into the drive, I heard a door slam and a minute later the front door rattled as Sally tried to open it. A minute later the same thing happened at the back door. Another minute went by and then the doorbell rang. I ignored it and it rang again and then again. Finally Sally started pounding on the door and I got up and went and opened it.

"What do you want?"

"I want to come in."

"I don't think so. I don't have any room in my house for a cheating bitch."

"What the hell are you talking about?"

"Just leave, Sally. Go and party with your new friends."

"Oh come on baby, all I did was try some shock therapy on you. I thought maybe that might get you back to functioning again."

"Nice try Sally, but I don't believe you. I'll move your shit out of the house and into the driveway tomorrow," and I started to close the door on her.

"Let me in, damn it!"

"No Sally, I am not letting you in."

"Where am I supposed to go this time of night?"

"Not my problem, Sally. You were the one who said you weren't coming home with me. Go find your three friends; maybe they will let you stay with them."

I closed the door in her face and went into the living room and sat down to wait for the next act. Sally beat on the door, cussed and hollered until the neighbors got tired of the racket and called the cops. They knocked on the door and asked me what the problem was, and I told them I'd locked her out for cheating on me with other men. Sally loudly denied cheating on me and the cops asked me to let her in and then work on the problem come daylight.

"The only way she is getting into this house is with a court order."

The cop shrugged and told Sally it was a civil matter and she would need to get an attorney. Then they offered to drop her at a motel. She said okay and they left.

Everything to that point was an act to buy time. Now that Sally was gone I figured that I had until noon the next day to do what I was going to do. By seven I had cancelled all of our credit cards; by nine I had cleaned out all the checking and savings accounts; and by ten I had rented a U-Haul truck. By twelve I had everything I wanted moved out of the house and placed in storage; and by one I was checked into a motel on the other side of town.

The house was mortgaged to the hilt with a first and second mortgage so Sally could have it for all that I cared. I wouldn't make any more payments on it and she didn't make enough at her job to make the payments, so it would end up going into foreclosure. That would hurt my credit, but before it happens I would trade in the car for a new one, get a couple of credit cards in my name only and my credit check would still show good when I found an apartment to rent.

Sally called my cell half a dozen times on Saturday, but I didn't take the calls. She got through to me once by using a number I didn't recognize, but as soon as I heard her voice I hung up on her. She called me eleven times Sunday and I ignored her. Monday, when I got off work, I found her sitting on the hood of my car when I got to the parking lot. She started right in on me.

"Don't you think that you are being just a little unreasonable?"

"No, I don't. Actually I'm quite proud of the way I handled it. I didn't get violent at all."

"You had no reason to get violent and you had no reason to lock me out of the house. I didn't do anything. All I did was try to see if I could jog something that would get you back in operation. I was desperate, baby. Fourteen months with no sex was killing me. Maybe what I tried to do seems a little drastic too you, but I swear to you honey, I did not do anything with those guys."

"Sorry Sally, but I don't believe you."

"You said you were going to put my things out in the driveway."

"I changed my mind. I moved out of the house; you can have it."

"You moved out? Why did you do that? When?"

"Saturday. I moved out because the house is too big for me to live in alone."

"Why didn't you answer my calls and tell me that, instead of letting me waste money on a motel room that I can't afford?"

"I didn't take your calls because I didn't want to talk to you and I don't care if you can afford motel rooms or not."

"We can't settle this if we don't talk."

"As far as I'm concerned it is settled. You stuck it to me and now you can color me gone."

She stared at me for a couple of moments and then said, "I can see that I'll have to leave you alone for a couple of days so you can cool down. I'll call you on Wednesday," and she turned to leave.

I smiled as I thought, "Oh no you won't missy, you'll be calling me a lot sooner than that." Two hours later my cell phone rang. I looked at the display and saw it was Sally. I'd been expecting the call so I answered:

"What do you want?"

"What did you do? The motel won't accept my credit cards. They say I'm being declined."

"No surprise there since I cancelled them all so I wouldn't be responsible for your debts. I wouldn't write them a check either if I were you."

"Why? What did you do?"

"Cleaned out the checking account."

"What am I supposed to do?"

"To quote Clark Gable, 'Frankly, I don't give a damn!'" and I hung up on her.

Monday evening I found an apartment close to work and Tuesday I moved in. My cell rang constantly Tuesday and most of Wednesday and I finally turned it off. Wednesday when I got off work, I found Sally waiting for me in the parking lot again.

"Have you calmed down yet? Can we put this silly misunderstanding behind us? Come on home honey, it is where you belong."

"No misunderstanding on my part, Sally. I understood you perfectly when you said you weren't going home with me and when I left, sure enough, you didn't leave with me."

"What do I have to do to convince you that I didn't do anything?"

"I don't know. Maybe you could ask your three friends to come see me, look me in the eye and then tell me that nothing happened."

"I don't know where to find them. They were just guys I met at the bar."

I knew better – I'd heard her tell one of them to call her at work, and I knew that since he had nailed her once, he would be calling her to see if he could get some more. So I said, "Not my problem, Sally. You made the mess, you clean it up."

I got in my car and drove away.

Three weeks went by with Sally calling me almost daily trying to get me to come home; and every day I said the same thing.

"I haven't heard from your lovers yet."

"God damn it! They are not and never were my lovers."

"Okay then, I still haven't heard from your one night stands," and I'd hang up.

It was the Thursday of the fifth week since I'd moved out when she called me and told me that she had finally found them. Bill is a long-haul trucker and he is on a run right now and won't be back for two weeks. Art is out of town working on a construction project and won't be back for another three or maybe four weeks. The only one I could get in touch with was Dan.

"Where can we meet?"

"It started at the Landing Strip, so I'll meet him there."

"What time do you want us to be there?"

"Just him, Sally. I don't want you there sending him signals when I ask questions. Tell him to make it tomorrow at eight."

***

The next night at eight, I was sitting at a table when he came in. He was the one I had watched fuck Sally. He looked around, saw me and headed for the table and sat down. The waitress was there as soon as he was so he ordered and then said:

"I understand that you and your wife are having problems."

"You could say that."

"She says you wanted to talk to me."

"Wrong. What I told her was that I didn't believe her story and she asked me how she could prove to me that she wasn't lying. I told her that if she could get the three of you to look me straight in the eye and back her story up, I might – just might – listen to her. So, I don't want to talk to you, she wants you to talk to me."

"Same thing."

"All depends on your point of view."

"So what do we do?"

"I want you to look me right in the eye and tell me what happened."

"Not much. She told us you were having an argument and she wanted to rub your nose the wrong way to piss you off. I guess she did that, huh?"

"Go on."

"That's it. She told you she wasn't going home with you and that she was going to party with us. You left. We had a few more drinks, danced a couple of more dances and then I ran her home."

"That's it?"

"That's all of it."

And he said it all with a straight face. If I hadn't seen him with my own eyes, I would probably have believed him.

"That help any?"

"I've still got to talk to the other two."

"Why? They will just say the same thing."

"All I know is what you are telling me you saw. Now that I've heard your story I'll have questions for the other two. I'll talk to them separately and ask each of them different questions and then compare stories. If I can convince myself that Sally didn't cheat, we can start talking again. Thanks for stopping by."

"Glad to be of help."

I headed on back to my apartment and before I got there my cell went off and when I answered it was Sally.

"Did you talk to him?"

"Yes."

"And?"

"And what?"

"Are you going to come home?"

"Not yet. I still have the other two to talk to yet."

"Come on honey, they are going to say the same thing, nothing happened."

"I still have to talk to them. Maybe Dan is a practiced liar and he was able to fool me and maybe the other two aren't as good at lying and I'll be able to tell."

"Honey, I need you to come home. Things are going to hell

without you here. I got a notice from the mortgage company that we are behind on the house payment. I don't make enough to make the payments on the house and keep the phone, lights and gas turned on. You need to come home baby; we need to put this mess behind us. You keep playing this game baby, and we could end up losing the house."

"All things you should have thought of Sally, when you were playing your games. I would have thought that you would have known me well enough to know how I would respond to what you did. I keep telling you Sally, you made this mess and you get to be the one to clean it up. I told you what you had to do to try and clean it up. Until I talk to the other two guys nothing is going to change. Don't bother calling me again until you have the other two available for me to talk with.

**

It was three weeks before she called me and told me Bill was back in town. I told her to have him meet me at the Strip the next night at eight. I met Bill and it was a repeat of my meeting with Dan; except Bill couldn't lie for shit. I listened to what he had to say, acted like I believed it, finished my beer and went on home to my apartment. I was no sooner in the door and Sally was on the phone.

"Are you going to come home now?"

"I still have one more to talk to. Let me know when you have him available," and I hung up on her.

One week later she called me and told me that Art, the last of the three, was back and I made arrangements to meet him two nights later at the Landing Strip. I got the same story from him that I got from Bill and Dan and he was no better a liar than Bill; but I let on as if he had convinced me that they really hadn't done anything. I wasn't even out of the bar parking lot when Sally had me on the phone.

"Are you satisfied now?"

"I guess. They are either very good liars, or you really didn't do anything. I just need one more thing."

"What?"

"I need you to go get tested for STDs. I'm not taking any chances."

"Damn it, you are being totally unreasonable."

"Maybe so Sally, but it is my life and I'm not going to gamble with it. Get tested and then call me.

Sally called me two weeks later and told me she had the lab results and I told her to fax them to me. She did and the tests said she was clean, but I knew that HIV could take six or eight months to show up. I could milk things for several more months, but I didn't want to run things out that long. Ten minutes after I received the fax, she called me and asked me if I'd gotten it and I said that I had.

"Please come home."

"Give me a day or two to think on it."

"We are running out of time. I've got overdue notices from both the first and second mortgage companies. We are already two months behind on the first."

"I get the feeling Sally that you don't really want me so much as you want a bill payer back in the house."

"That's not true. I miss you and I need you with me. Life sucks with you gone."

"Then a day or two for me to finally get my head together isn't going to hurt now, is it? Call me on Tuesday."

I spent the weekend on the beach watching all the little honeys run around in their skimpy bikinis and Good God Almighty – Mr. Happy was back!

***

Sally called me on Tuesday. "Are you coming home?"

"Yes, I'll come home. I've got a busy week here at work so I won't be able to do it until the weekend. I'll be there Saturday."

"Thank God! I'll make it up to you baby, I swear to God I'll make it up to you."

The rest of the week went fast and Friday I packed a bag, turned my cell phone off and spent another weekend at the beach. I turned my cell back on when I got to work on Monday and it was no sooner on when I got a call from Sally.

"What happened? Where were you?"

"I went to the beach this weekend."

"You said you were coming home."

"Yeah, well, I thought about that and I decided I need one more thing to set my mind to rest."

"What *now* for God's sake?"

"It has been what, a little over three months since you told me to go on home alone so you could party with your three friends? I think I want to wait six more months and make sure you don't have a baby."

There was silence on the other end for several seconds and then she said:

"You bastard. Why are you doing this to me?"

"What? Wanting to make sure that you aren't pregnant? I'm doing that for *me* Sally, not for you. I've got to get back to work," and I disconnected.

I smiled and pushed a preset number and when the other party answered, I told them I was ready.

***

That night when I got off work, I found a very angry Sally waiting for me in the parking lot.

"What the fuck is this?" She yelled waving a handful of papers at me.

"What is what Sally?"

"These divorce papers. What the fuck are you doing?"

"Stupid question Sally, especially since you have the answer to your question right there in your hand. I'm divorcing you. The papers say irreconcilable differences, but we both know the real reason is infidelity, don't we?"

"Damn it, I didn't do anything. Why can't you get that through your head?"

"Because I know you are lying through your teeth Sally. I didn't just leave and go home that night. I moved the car across the street, parked and waited to see what you would do. I watched you do those three assholes in that car. I was standing there watching and listening. I was there when Dan asked you when he could do you again, and I heard you tell him to call you at work and that you would arrange a long lunch hour."

Her face paled and I saw her finally accept that she was busted.

"So if you knew, why didn't you say something so we could have worked things out?"

"What's to work out Sally?"

"Honey, it was a mistake. A big mistake, and a stupid one. But it didn't mean anything. None of those three clowns meant anything to me. I love you and you should know it. I didn't think you would really leave me there. I knew you would be outside waiting for me and a couple of minutes after you left I came out to get in the car with you. I looked all over the parking lot and I couldn't believe it when I didn't find you there. I went back inside and tried to talk the guys into giving me a ride home, but they said they wouldn't unless I had a couple more drinks and danced some more with them.

"Honey, I hadn't been laid in over fourteen months and I was hurting. Add to that too much to drink and I did a stupid thing. And yes, I told Dan he could call me at work, but I didn't mean it. I had to stay on his good side until he gave me a ride home. I didn't keep in touch with any of them honey, that's why it took me so long to get to them to talk to you.

"I've regretted it every minute of every day since. Honest to God baby, I'm sorry and I'll do anything to make it up to you. I know now that trying to shock you was a stupid idea, but that is all I set out to do honey, please, you have to believe me."

"It doesn't matter anymore, Sally. You fucked three guys after telling me to take off without you and I'll never forget that. Even if I could forgive, I could never forget and I would see it in my mind every time I see you and there isn't any way I can live with that."

"So if you had already decided that you were going to kick me to the curb, why did you put me through the last three months?"

"I had to do something to get back at you. I needed to string you along long enough to see to it that you got hosed in the divorce."

"Hosed? What does that mean?"

"This is a no fault state Sally. That means that in a divorce, all property gets split 50/50. All we have is the house and I've dragged things out long enough that unless you can quickly find yourself a sugar daddy, the house will go into foreclosure. Fifty percent of nothing is nothing Sally. But hey, you still have your three asshole buddies you can party with so it isn't a total loss. Take care Sally, and have a nice life. Hope I never see you again."

I got in my car and drove off.

End of the 4th Story

———✄———

Chuck's Mistake

My marriage is over. I knew what I did was wrong and I did it anyway. I could have said no, but I didn't. I learned later that there were external forces at play, but that doesn't change the fact that I could have avoided it all if I had but chosen to do so. My big crime? I let my dick make a decision for me.

***

Ellie and I had been sweethearts from the seventh grade on. I was her first and only boyfriend. We went steady through junior high and high school and I proposed on the day we graduated. Ellie said yes and then we found out that things were not all that simple. Both sets of parents were against our getting married and it wasn't because my parents didn't like Ellie or her parents didn't like me; it was because they felt we were too young and that we needed to wait until we had gotten through college. Ellie's parents worked hard on her and mine worked just as hard on me; and in the end they got what they wanted.

Ellie went off to Eastern Michigan to get her degree and I went to U of M to get mine. We didn't expect it to be a major problem because the two schools were less than thirty miles apart. We talked to each other almost every day and we saw each other on weekends. But being apart after being together for so long altered the relationship. It was my first time away from Ellie. There had never been another girl in my life because Ellie was always there.

The first couple of months at Michigan were spent finding out where things were and getting settled in. I was in constant touch with Ellie by phone, but eventually I began to notice the girls that I was attending classes with; and being a horny young guy who was missing his regular pussy, (yes - Ellie and I had consummated our relationship -

many times over) I could not help but look at some of them and wonder if making it with them would be different than making it with Ellie. Wondering is all I probably would have done had not some of those girls done some wondering of their own.

It was a Monday and I was attending a mixer at the Delta Omega house. I'd had a half a dozen beers and was feeling pretty mellow when a girl who was in my English Lit 101 class pulled me into a corner and started kissing me. I swear to God, she was the aggressor all the way, but as a young horny guy, was I going to push her away? Not fucking hardly!

"I wondered what it would be like to kiss you," she said. "Are you any good in bed?"

How in the hell are you supposed to answer a question like that if you are a guy? Only one way! "I've not had any complaints," I said, which was true because I'd only ever had sex with Ellie and she had never complained.

"Well, let us just see." She took me by the hand and led me off to a bedroom.

Now, Ellie had been my only experience, but I wanted to show this girl I could live up to my boast, and the only way I could think of doing that was to make it last for a while. I spent a lot of time on foreplay, including eating her pussy, and then I took my time fucking her. I wanted to get off in the worst way, but I forced myself to go slow and take my time. She was yelling at me to go faster, do it harder and push it deep, but I ignored her and as a result she had three orgasms before I finally couldn't hold back any longer. She lay there looking up at me and then said:

"I'm taking you home with me."

Home was a three bedroom house that she shared with five other girls. We did it twice more that night and then fell asleep together. I woke up alone in the morning and got up and dressed. I went down the stairs and into a living room where four almost-naked females were bustling about getting ready to get dressed. All of them had panties on and three of them were wearing bras, but the fourth, a rather striking redhead, was bare breasted. None of them paid any attention to me or made any effort to cover up. In fact, the redhead just stood there so I could feast my eyes on her tits, and I knew she was doing it deliberately because I could see her nipples stiffen. A little blond came up to me and said:

"Debbie had an early class and she said to tell you that she would meet you at the library at three."

I spent the next three nights in Debbie's bed. On Friday morning I woke up to a blow job and when I looked, I saw that it wasn't Debbie – it was the redhead. By the end of my freshman year, I had screwed all five of the girls sharing that house and not a one of them cared that I was doing the other four also.

I spent the weekends with Ellie trying to fuck me to death and the week nights with Debbie or one of her roommates trying to do the same thing. Eventually my grades began to suffer and I was on the ragged edge of flunking out, so I ended up cutting back on the nights I spent with Debbie and the rest of the girls in the house. I started my sophomore year determined that my classes would take priority. By mid-point of my soph year, three of the five girls had dropped out of school and only Debbie and Alice (the redhead) were still around. The two of them became my 'steadies' until the start of my junior year when Debbie didn't return to school following spring break. Alice was my main squeeze through the balance of my junior year, but she didn't return to school at the start of our senior year.

I mention all this because it played a major part in the disaster. It gave me an unrealistic mind set. I saw what the five girls were doing and what other girls were doing; I saw what the guys I knew were doing and I knew what I was doing – and I assumed that Ellie was doing the same over at Eastern Michigan. We never talked about things like that when we were together; I just assumed that she was sowing her wild oats and getting it out of her system just as I was. The others meant nothing to me; I was totally in love with Ellie and from what I saw, Ellie was totally in love with me.

Graduation came and Ellie and I found work in our chosen fields. Ellie and her mother began planning the wedding. Six months after our graduation, Ellie and I were married and we set up housekeeping.

***

Did you ever know someone that you didn't care for, but didn't know why? That is how I felt about Sonia. Sonia was a girl that Ellie met in her freshman year at EMU. They became close friends and they stayed close after graduation. She was an extremely sexy looking lady. She had a nice personality and a great sense of humor, but whenever I was around her I felt bad vibes. If only there was something definite, I could have gone to Ellie and said:

"I don't like her and I don't want her around and here is why."

But there wasn't any way I could go to Ellie and say that I didn't want her around because she gives off bad vibes. She was Ellie's close friend and I was just going to have to live with it. Ellie and Sonia worked fairly close to each other, so they had lunch together two or three times a week, and at least once a week they met for a drink or two after work.

A couple of years went by and then one Monday night, at a birthday party for a friend held at a local lounge, my life changed – and not for the better. The drinks were flowing, the music was loud and I was having a blast. I'd had enough to drink that I was having a great time, but not thinking too clearly. Sonia came up to me and pulled me out onto the dance floor.

I did mention that Sonia was a sexy lady, right? Well, she

plastered herself against me, rubbed her tits into my chest, pushed her leg against my cock and kept it there. When the music stopped, she pulled me against her and kissed me hard. She shoved her tongue in my mouth and after a long kiss, she pulled me off the dance floor and along behind her out into the parking lot. Every ten feet or so she would stop and give me another long kiss with lots of tongue action, rub my cock through my pants and then pull me another ten feet or so and do it again.

My head wasn't all that clear and my cock was trying to bust out of my trousers. Even though I wasn't thinking all that clearly, I knew that I shouldn't be letting Sonia do what she was doing. I *knew*, but my cock was straining to be set free and the blood that my brain needed to properly function was in my dick. Sonia was pulling me along saying:

"Hurry Chuck, hurry. I've wanted this since I met you and this is my chance."

She finally got me to her car, pulled me inside and then pushed me down on my back on the rear seat. She unzipped me, pulled out my cock and then crawled on top of me. "Oh God baby, I want this, I really want this," she said as she took hold of my cock, lined it up with her pussy and then sat down on it. I lay there looking up at her as she fucked herself on my erection and thinking, "This is wrong. I shouldn't be doing this. It just isn't right," but I made no attempt to push Sonia off me. She was pulling up and then driving down hard on me and moaning:

"So good, so good baby; I should have done this long ago. Cum for momma baby, come for momma."

As much as I'd had to drink, I wasn't going to be cumming anytime soon; and that seemed to suit Sonia, as she pounding down on me and had orgasm after orgasm. I have no idea how long we were at it before she screamed out loud:

"Oh God yes!"

And then she collapsed on my chest and moaned, "Again baby, I want to go again. Give me just a minute to get my breath back."

As she lay on top of me breathing hard, I finally woke up to the fact that I needed to get her off of me and get away from her, but as soon as I had that thought I heard:

"God damn you Chuck! How could you do this to me?"

I looked over Sonia's shoulder and saw Ellie standing outside the car looking in. Sonia scrambled to get off of me and then went running after Ellie, leaving me in the car and feeling like shit. I got myself together and headed for the lounge to face the music. On the way I met Ellie and Sonia coming out. Ellie gave me a dirty look and said:

"I'll be staying with Sonia. I really don't want to talk to you or have anything to do with you right now."

I stood there numb as I watched the two of them walk to Sonia's car, get in and drive away.

***

I woke up the next morning with the mother of all hangovers. I was alone in the bed so I dragged myself out and headed for the kitchen to see if Ellie had the coffee on. It wasn't until I walked into the room that I remembered that Ellie wasn't there. And then I remembered why.

I put the coffee on, called in sick to work and then sat down at the kitchen table and stared at the wall. Why in God's name had I done what I did last night? I was in deep shit and I knew it and I didn't know how I was going to get out of it. I had no defense. All I could do was say that I was sorry and that I had been drunk and didn't know what I was doing, but that would be a lie and I had never been very good when it came to lying to Ellie. It was true that I had been drinking excessively, but I knew what was happening and I knew it was wrong and I hadn't fought it. I knew that if I hadn't been drinking that it never would have happened, but that was scant consolation.

After six cups of coffee and after looking at it from every angle imaginable, I realized that my only hope was to get down on my knees and beg for forgiveness. It took me until two in the afternoon to work up the courage to call Ellie at work. As soon as she heard my voice, she said:

"I don't want to talk to you right now and I don't want you bothering me. I'll call you when I feel I'm ready to talk," and then she hung up on me.

Okay, I thought, maybe a cooling off period would be a good thing. I managed to survive Tuesday and I went into work on Wednesday, expecting that I would hear from Ellie when I got home that night, but she didn't call. A half a dozen times I caught myself reaching for the phone, and in each time I talked myself out of picking it up and calling her. Best let her make the first move, I told myself; don't push her.

I don't know exactly when I started to feel uneasy. It was probably Wednesday night when I got ready for bed or it may have been Thursday morning when I was getting ready for work. What it was that started the feeling didn't register until halfway through the day on Thursday, and then I began to have some very unsettling thoughts. When I got home that night, the first thing I did was head for the bathroom and open the medicine cabinet. Nothing of Ellie's was in the cabinet. I looked at the counter-top and noticed that all of Ellie's cosmetics were gone. A check of her closet showed that some of her clothes were gone. Had Ellie come home while I had been at work? I didn't think so. In fact, the more I thought about it, the more I was sure that the bathroom counter-top had been bare on Tuesday morning. Had the clothes been gone on Tuesday too? Had she packed them and taken them out of the house on Monday?

The more I thought about it the more the fog cleared away. I had been so busy feeling guilty and feeling sorry for myself that I had not been thinking straight. Ellie catches her best friend fucking me and she walks out on me and goes home with the woman I cheated with? Something didn't add up and I was getting a very bad feeling.

I picked up the phone and called Sonia's, but got no answer. I tried several more times and still got no answer. I got up early on Friday and called. Sonia answered and I asked for Ellie, and Sonia told me that Ellie didn't want to talk with me, and then she hung up. At nine I called Ellie at work and as soon as she heard my voice she said:

"Damn it Chuck, I told you not to bother me. I'll call you when I'm ready to talk to you."

"Ellie, we have some major problems here and we need to talk about them now."

"When I'm ready, Chuck. Not until I'm ready," and she hung up on me again.

I was starting to get pissed. Nothing about what was going on smelled right. I decided: to hell with talking on the phone. I left work early and drove over to where Ellie worked. Her normal quitting time was five and when five-thirty came around and she still hadn't come out of the building, I went inside to find her. She wasn't there and I was told she had left work early. I drove over to Sonia's but there was nobody there – and that did it for me. I called Ellie's cell phone and got no answer, so I left a message on her voice mail and told her that if she didn't call and talk to me or come home by nine that night, she wouldn't have a home to come home to. Then I went home to wait.

Nine o'clock came and went with no Ellie and no phone call, so I grabbed a couple of suitcases and boxes and started packing. By eleven I had everything out of the apartment that I wanted. I tossed my wedding ring onto the middle of the kitchen table, locked up the place and left. Drastic? Maybe, but the whole situation stunk to high heaven. There was something rotten in Denmark when she could move in with the woman she caught me doing the nasty with but would not even talk to me, and I was not – was not! – going to let myself be played for a fool. I turned my cell phone off, checked into a motel and went to bed.

***

I got up Saturday, had breakfast at a Denny's and then went looking for an apartment close to where I work. I hit half a dozen, found one that I liked and signed a lease. I hit a used furniture store to get what I needed and started to move in. I hit Denny's again for my evening meal, caught a movie and then went home to my new apartment. I got there about ten-thirty and I figured by then Ellie might have gone home or tried to call. I turned my cell phone back on with the intention of giving her a taste of her own medicine: if she called, I'd tell her that I didn't want to talk to her and hang up.

The cell phone went off at three in the morning. It was Sonia calling to tell me that Ellie was in the hospital. I asked what was wrong with her and Sonia told me that she had been raped.

When I walked into the hospital's emergency room waiting room, Sonia saw me and jumped up and ran over to me. She was crying and it looked like she had been for some time. I asked where Ellie was and she told me that Ellie was in one of the treatment rooms in the back. I started to go back there but she stopped me. She told me that the police were with her and they didn't want anyone back there until they were done talking with her.

"What happened?" Sonia started crying again. "For God's sake Sonia, stop the sniveling and tell me what happened."

All that did was make her cry harder. I was about to walk away from her and go find somebody who could tell me something, when in a tear-filled voice Sonia sobbed out:

"Oh God, I never meant for this to happen. I'm sorry, oh God, I'm so sorry. I never should have done it. It's all my fault. I'm sorry, oh God I'm just so sorry."

"You never should have done what, Sonia? What did you do?"

More crying and more boo-hooing – until I finally lost it. "God damn it Sonia, what happened?!!! If you don't stop the damned sniveling and tell me what is going on, I swear to God I'll wrap my hands around your throat and shake you to death!"

Before she could say anything, two men walked into the room, saw me with Sonia and came over to us and asked me if I was Ellie's husband. I told them I was, and they identified themselves as detectives Stoner and Monroe. Detective Stoner asked me what I could tell him about my wife's activities for the last two or three days and I told him that I didn't have a clue; that she had walked out on me Monday and had refused to talk to me since. Then I asked them what was going on.

"I can't find out what happened. Sonia can't stop crying long enough to talk and I was told I couldn't see Ellie until you were done with her."

The two men looked at each other and some sort of communication took place between them. Then Stoner shrugged his shoulders and nodded. Monroe said:

"Let's go to the hospital cafeteria and get some coffee and we will tell you what we know."

At 0145 Sonia had placed a 911 call and reported a woman being held against her will and being raped. Two officers were dispatched on the call and when they arrived at the address given, they found eleven men in a room with a naked female. They called for back-up as the eleven men scattered and two more squad cars arrived. By then they had gotten a good look at Ellie and had called the paramedics, who arrived and immediately transported Ellie to the hospital.

Monroe and Stoner had been assigned the case and they had come to the hospital and interviewed Sonia and Ellie. The story, as they had pieced it together, was that Sonia and Ellie had gone to the Aladdin

Lounge on Friday night for drinks and dancing. Sometime during the course of the evening, Ellie had been given a date rape drug and sometime around 11 PM, while Sonia was out on the dance floor, a couple of men had taken Ellie out to the parking lot and had sex with her in the back of a van. Word got around and several more men visited the van and it was decided that rather than risk the cops being called, they would take Ellie to an apartment. Once there, she was sexually used until Sonia placed the 911 call.

"Friday night? Until a quarter of two tonight? It took Sonia over 24 hours to call 911?"

"Apparently, Miss Talbot thought that your wife had left on her own accord. She didn't become worried until your wife failed to return to Miss Talbot's apartment the next day."

"She thought Ellie had left on her own?"

"According to Miss Talbot, they had gone to Aladdin's to look for men to pick up. She thought your wife had 'scored,' as she put it. It wasn't until 6 PM on Saturday evening that she became worried and went looking for your wife. She found someone who had heard that some guys had a bar pick-up that they had been partying with all day Saturday. Miss Talbot got an address, went over and saw what was happening and then she placed the 911 call."

"Sonia told you that? She said that they had gone to that lounge looking for guys to pick up?"

Monroe nodded his head yes. I sat there and stared at them for maybe thirty seconds and then Stoner said that the doctor had sedated Ellie after their interview, and that I probably wouldn't be able to talk to her until in the morning. After they left, I sat there staring down into my coffee cup. It was maybe twenty minutes before I got up and went back to the waiting room. Sonia was still sitting there and I went over to her, took her by the arm, and then I pulled her up off her seat.

"What are you doing?"

"You and I are going out to get a breath of fresh air," and then I pulled her along behind me out into the parking lot. I pulled her along to my car and then I pushed her inside and got in behind her.

"I want to know what is going on Sonia. I want to know it all and you are going to tell me, or I swear to God I'll put you into the hospital bed next to Ellie and the two of you can share a hospital room together."

Could I have hurt her? I doubt it, but she didn't know that and the story came out. It happened on one of the nights that she and Ellie had stopped for drinks after work. They had been sitting there drinking when a girl who had known Sonia in high school had come over and joined them. Ellie was introduced and then the girl and Sonia played "catch up." Long story short, it turns out that the girl went to U of M, knew me and on hearing Ellie's last name she asked Ellie if we were related. Before Ellie could answer, Sonia told the girl no; that it was just a coincidence.

Sonia knew that the girl was a slut in high school and figured that she probably was one in college. Sonia also knew that I didn't really care for her and if a slut like the girl knew me at U of M, there was probably some dirt there that she could use to rub my nose in. Several drinks and some prying got the girl to talking about me and the five girls who shared the house.

Ellie was pissed. It turned out that while I was sowing my wild oats and thinking that Ellie was sowing hers, she wasn't. Ellie had stayed 'true' to me and finding out that I hadn't stayed 'true' to her angered her and Sonia gleefully took advantage of that anger. She went to work on Ellie to try and convince her she needed to get even with me for my 'betrayal' and she finally convinced Ellie to do it. They spent a couple of weeks thinking of what to do and what they did to me was the plan they came up with: get me drunk, let Ellie catch Sonia and me, and then use that as an excuse to let Ellie go out and sample a few cocks; and after she'd had a few she would come back to me, tell me she loved me enough to forgive my indiscretion with Sonia.

"She was willing to let you fuck me just so she could go out and fuck strangers?"

"I wasn't supposed to fuck you. I was supposed to yell out once I got your cock out of your pants and she would run up and go through her act."

"Why did you change the plan and fuck me?"

"I wasn't lying when I said I had wanted you since the first time I saw you. I knew that you would never give me a tumble and that my only chance would be when I had you on your back on that seat – and so I took it."

"And Ellie didn't get pissed at you when you didn't stick to the plan?"

"She doesn't know. She saw me on top of you, but she couldn't see that you were in me and I told her you were trying to get in, but that I kept moving so you couldn't find the hole."

I sat there and stared at her. I had no trouble believing what she told me, but I still had a hard time accepting it. "And I was just supposed to say, 'Glad to have you home dear. Did you satisfy your craving?'"

"You were never supposed to know about the men. All you were supposed to do was think that she was too pissed at you to talk to you or want to be around you for a couple of days."

I stared at her and something told me that I hadn't heard it all. "You are holding something back Sonia. I can tell that you haven't told me all of it."

She looked away and then said, "We went out Tuesday,

Wednesday and Thursday and picked up guys. Friday was supposed to be the last time and then she was going to come home and tell you that she forgave you."

"So she was deliberately a whore on Tuesday, Wednesday and Thursday and she was going to be one again on Friday?"

"Oh come on Chuck; what's the big deal? You had your fun so she wanted to have a little fun too. It didn't change anything – she still loves you."

"Yeah Sonia, but just not enough to remember her wedding vows. You know, the part about forsaking all others? What I did was done before we got married. With the exception of how you two set me up, I have been a faithful husband and I expected to be able to say the same about my wife. If she wanted to play then she should have done it before she walked down the aisle at our wedding."

"What are you going to do?"

"I've already done it. I gave her a deadline for talking with me and when she didn't meet it I moved out. I'll be seeing a divorce lawyer sometime next week."

"Don't do that to her Chuck, she loves you."

"But not enough Sonia, not near enough or she wouldn't have pulled shit like this on me."

I got out of the car and went back into the hospital. Ellie was still on my insurance so I went to the admissions desk and gave them the necessary information. Then I went back to my apartment and went to bed. Sunday I got two calls from Ellie and one from Sonia and I hung up on both of them.

***

Monday I went to work and around ten I got a call from Sonia and I took it. "Ellie has been trying to get to you. She needs to talk to you Chuck. Don't you think you should at least come and see her?"

"No Sonia, it is way too late for that now."

"What should I tell her?"

"I don't know Sonia. Maybe you can discuss your marvelous plan and talk about how well it worked. She certainly got to experience a bunch of other cocks and that is what you both wanted, right?"

I hung up and went back to work. They kept Ellie for two more days for observation. Mentally, Ellie was a wreck. I'm told that she would flinch and cower every time a man came near her. They ended up posting a notice on her room door that male orderlies were not allowed in the room and that the male doctor had to be replaced by a female one. Thursday Sonia called me and told me Ellie was being released.

"Why tell me?"

"So you can pick her up and take her home."

"No thanks Sonia. In the first place, her home and my home aren't the same place any more. She had no problem in walking out on me and staying at your place, so you pick her up and take her home with you."

***

I saw a lawyer and petitioned for a divorce and six months later I was a free man. During the six month wait for the petition to be granted, everyone on Ellie's side of the family and everyone (except my father) on my side worked at trying to get me to forgive Ellie and get back together with her. The consensus was that I was an insensitive brute.

"My gosh, the poor girl was raped. Where is your compassion?"

They all totally overlooked the fact that Ellie had set herself up as a target. She might as well have been wearing a sign that said, "Pick me, pick me." I told them all that if Ellie had been at a party, gotten drunk and been taken advantage of, or if she had been dragged into an alley and assaulted, there might have been room for compassion and forgiveness. But Ellie went out deliberately looking for cock and it was her own damned fault that she got more than she expected.

There were other issues that everybody seemed to overlook. Who can say that all of the social diseases that Ellie ended up infected with came from her weekend gang bang? They could just as easily have been picked up from her one night stands on Tuesday, Wednesday and Thursday. If Friday had gone as she had planned – another one nighter – she was all set to come home to me, say "I forgive you" and then climb in bed and share with me everything she had picked up. Thank you, but no thank you. I did not need someone like that in my life.

Would I miss her? Of course I would. Ellie had been a part of my life for over half of it and it would be a long time, if ever, before I got over her; but there was no way I could live with someone who did what she had done.

=Epilogue=

Ellie made at least two dozen more attempts to try and get me to talk to her and I refused. I finally sent her a letter fully explaining my position on the matter and told her that there was absolutely no chance I would ever accept her again. The phone calls stopped and Ellie made no further attempts to contact me.

The police were able to identify the man who they thought slipped Ellie the date rape drug and they made an arrest, but the man beat the rap. The only witness who could state positively that the man doped Ellie's drink had taken off and without his testimony, that part of the case fell apart. On the rape charge, the man swore that Ellie had been absolutely willing; and the testimony of a dozen other witnesses, stating that Ellie had been in the bar picking up men on other nights that week, won him a "Not guilty" verdict.

It is still too soon to tell if Ellie contracted HIV, but she had caught damn near everything else. Her cunt was a regular Petri dish of organisms. The police and the medical personnel at the hospital estimated that between thirty-five and forty-five men had used Ellie from the time she left the Aladdin until the police responded to the 911 call.

Ellie had to quit her job because of being scared when she was around men. She moved in with Sonia who, to her credit, stepped up to the plate where Ellie was concerned. She took her in and is supporting her while Ellie is in therapy. Hopefully the doctors will help Ellie get past her aversion to men and she will be able to get on with her life.

End of the 5th Story

———✂———

Sandra's Accident

One of life's great mysteries, I thought, as I sat waiting for the light to change. Why was the light here? I stopped for it at an average of ten times a week and at various times of the day and night; and ninety percent of the time there was never another vehicle in sight. Whatever traffic, I saw the other ten percent wasn't enough to justify a four way stop sign. So why was the light here when an inexpensive stop sign could have done the job?

The sudden shock of the hit drove all thoughts of traffic signals out of my mind and replaced them with bad thoughts: how bad was the damage, how much was my already too high insurance going to go up as a result. I was a little pissed when I got out of the van. I could understand a bumper tap when slowing and stopping, but I had been sitting still for almost a minute now. The woman who had hit me was probably wondering what the hell happened too. She was still sitting behind the wheel, face white and eyes wide open in shocked surprise and both hands gripping the steering wheel so hard that her knuckles were white. A quick glance at the back of the van showed no apparent damage, but I would need to look underneath to be sure.

The immediate problem seemed to be the woman in the car that hit me. Some of the color was returning to her face; she still had her death grip on the steering wheel, but her eyes were now closed and there were tears running down her cheeks. I walked up to her window and tapped on the glass, but she didn't move; she just sat there holding the steering wheel. I tried the door and it opened. "Lady, are you all right?" My words seemed to bring her out of her trance and she looked over at me with confusion on her face. I wasn't sure I should let her drive away even if there was no damage. She still hadn't answered me so I asked her again if she was all right.

"I'm okay. Just a little shook. I don't know what happened. I saw you, I was braking – I just don't know what happened."

"Well, we need to pull over to the side and stop blocking the road. Just pull through the light and park on the shoulder. I've got a cell phone so I'll call the cops and we can exchange information while we wait for them to get here."

I turned and started for the van and she cried, "Wait! Do we have to call the police? Can't we find some way to leave them out of it?"

I looked at her and wondered why she didn't want the cops involved. What did she have to hide?

"We can talk about it when we get out of the way of traffic," and I got in the van and pulled over on to the shoulder.

I took a quick look under the back of the van while I waited for her and everything looked okay. A quick look at the front end of her Expedition as she pulled up behind me showed no signs of damage. I had just about decided that it was in my best interest to say that everything was fine and just drive on. Even with no damage, a police report would still be on file, and the asshole insurance companies had access to those files and they could (and in fact did) use that information as an excuse to jack up your rates. That was when I had decided to drive off – until the woman got out of her car.

She was a knockout. Tall, about 5'9" with brown hair that fell down past her shoulders and a body to kill for. Her skirt was about six inches above her knees and as she walked toward me on four inch heels, I had a hard time tearing my eyes away from those legs to look at a chest that had to be at least a 36C. I made up my mind to stall because I didn't get to see anything this nice very often. I took out my wallet and dug out my driver's license and insurance card, but she showed no sign of doing the same as she walked up to me. She glanced at the front of her vehicle and at the back of mine and said, "There doesn't seem to be any damage. Can't we just forget the whole thing?"

"Well, I admit there doesn't seem to be anything wrong with the back of the van, but I have no idea what may be underneath."

I took my cell phone off my belt and made to look as if I was going to punch in a number. She reached out a hand and put it on my arm and said, "Don't, please don't."

"Lady, my insurance company requires an accident report before they pay any claim and that means I got to call the cops."

"No, you don't have to call the cops. I'll settle your insurance claim right here and now."

"Oh? And how do you propose to do that?"

She opened her purse and took out a checkbook. "I might be a woman, but I do know a little bit about some things. Your rear quarters are undamaged, the glass is all fine, and your bumper is straight. At the worst you have a bent bracket or the housing on your trailer plug is cracked. Five hundred should cover it and that is being overly generous."

Bear in mind that I was all for just driving off until she stepped out of the car, and the only reason I hadn't was because I liked looking at her; and I also admit that I was intrigued by the extent she seemed willing to go to in order to avoid the police. I decided to string it out.

"That may be true, but you will notice that the receiver tube of the trailer hitch sticks out past the bumper. What if that was pushed back and cracked the frame or cracked the hitch mount brackets? Lady, I don't know and the only way I'm going to find out is to get it looked at. And to have it looked at is going to cost and if it is damaged it will cost to get it fixed. That's why I have insurance, but the insurance won't pay without an accident report on file. To get it on file I have to call the cops," and I flipped the cover on the cell phone, not to call, but to see what she would do next.

"Please don't do that. How do you want to settle this between us right now?"

I looked at her and was trying to think of something to say when she said, "I saw the way you were looking at me when I was walking over here. I'll give you a check for five hundred and the best head you've ever had. In exchange – no cops."

To say I was stunned would be an understatement. I looked at her like she'd lost her mind and once again I wondered what she had to hide. I'm not a fool and my chance at something as nice as she was might never come again, so I took a chance. "The five, the head, and a piece of ass, plus I get to eat your pussy."

She looked at me for a moment and said, "Okay, but on the condition that you eat me after you fuck me."

I smiled and said, "Before and after."

She stuck out her hand and said, "Deal. Just let me check on my kids and make sure they are still sleeping," and she turned and went back to her car. She had kids in her car and she was willing to fuck me here and now? What was she? One of the ten most wanted?

"I hope you have padding in the back of your van."

I smiled as I opened the sliding side door, "Padding, carpet and an air mattress."

She looked at me and said, "You do this often?"

"Not with anybody who looks near as good as you do."

She gave me a dazzling smile, "Thank you." She climbed in the van and looked around.

"If you want more comfort, I only live half a mile from here."

"This is nice. I think it will work just fine," and she pulled her sweater off.

I had to revise my estimate of her bust size – closer to 38 than 36. She watched me watch her and she gave me a wicked grin, "Come on lover, show me what I have to work with."

We watched each other undress and I saw her eyebrows go up as my hard-on came out and I wondered what it meant: was I big to her or too small. What the hell, it didn't matter to me. What mattered to me was that for once in my life I was going to make love to a genuine sex goddess. Yes, I said make love. Looking at the perfection in front of me, I knew that just fucking her would be sacrilege. Suddenly I thought of something and I pulled my pants back on.

"What are you doing?"

I grabbed a box off one of the shelves attached to the side of the van and said, "Don't go away, I'll be right back." Two minutes later I was back in the van taking my pants off.

"What was that all about?"

I put a small box on the floor next to where we would be. "I'm an electronics salesman. That is a wireless baby monitor. If your kids wake up, you will hear them."

She gave me a strange look and then shrugged, "How do you want to do this?"

I looked at her and thought about my answer – god, but she was nice; no, she was *superb* – and then I said, "Given that the kids may wake up and you may have to leave before our deal is completely consummated, I want to go for what I want most right up front." She cocked her head and I could see a questioning look forming on her face.

"I want to eat you first."

"Why not go sixty-nine?" she asked. "That way you get to eat me and you get the head."

"No. In a sixty-nine half of my attention would be on what you were doing to me. I want all my attention on what I'm doing to you."

Again she gave me a strange look and then she shrugged and laid down on the air mattress. I have never, ever, before or since, tasted a sweeter pussy than hers. I nibbled, licked and sucked and made love to that hot hole for a good ten minutes. And it must have been good for her too because she had two orgasms and that was a first for me. I'd eaten a lot of pussy, but I'd never before had a woman cum because of it. I'd had plenty moan and say "oh yeah, like that" but not one bucking, screaming orgasm like this woman went through.

When she had stopped shaking, I rolled over and said, "Your turn." She got up on her knees, bent over and when her mouth closed on me, I actually groaned – it felt like feathers; hot wet feathers caressing my cock. She used her hands on my balls, teased my ass with her fingers, and made me want to cry over the fact that I'd never in my life had something that great and probably never would again. It didn't take her near as long to get me to the point of orgasm as it had taken me to get her to hers, and when I warned her I was about to cum, she took her mouth off me and said, "So?" and went back to sucking me. I mumbled something about some girls not wanting you to cum in their mouth, but she was already back at work and she didn't stop until my cock was limp.

She didn't even hesitate; she swung over me into a position for some sixty-nine and went to work on me again as I slid my tongue into her pussy. It took her two minutes to get me up again and then she moved again and mounted me. She no sooner had me all the way in her than the baby monitor started making noises. She looked at it and then back at me. I shrugged, "Go."

"Are you sure? It will be a little bit before they are fully awake."

"Kids come first," I said.

She gave me another strange look, the same as she had given me before, and then got off me and dressed. She got out her checkbook and said, "Who do I make it out to?"

I just shook my head and said, "You don't. It would have your name and address on it and I'd end up driving past your house two or three nights a week, staring at it and cursing my luck. Tell you what. Give me your panties and we will call it even."

Another one of her strange looks and then she said, "Are you from here? This planet, I mean? First you worry about my kids, and then you chose to satisfy me before letting me take care of you. You warn me when you are ready to cum in my mouth. You stop me from fucking you because one of my kids cries out in his sleep and now you want my undies instead of five hundred dollars. You are not a normal man."

I explained to her that I never intended to take her money or call the cops, but that I wasn't so stupid that I would turn down a chance at her. "Inside I'm crying my heart out. Just go, I don't want you to see a grown man cry."

Another long look and then she took off her panties and gave them too me. She bent down and kissed me and then she was gone.

***

Three weeks later I was sitting at a table at Sidney's, a fairly upscale restaurant, having lunch with a prospective client. He had called me and had asked me for a bid on a very large order. A very, very large order – one that would all by itself triple all the business I had done so far that year. I'd met Jack at his office and had made my pitch and then he had invited me to lunch. We sat down and ordered a cocktail and he said, "My wife is downtown shopping today and I asked her to join us. I hope you don't mind," and then he smiled, "Here she is now."

I turned my head and looked, and she looked every bit as magnificent as she had the day she had run into me. I stood up as she approached and tried to behave as if I had never seen her before. Jack introduced me to Sandra and I pulled out a chair for her. The three of us made small talk until the waiter took our order and then Jack excused himself to go and make a phone call. Sandra looked at me with an unsmiling face and said, "Is this where you tell me to find some way to make him give you his business or you'll make sure he finds out about me?"

I just shook my head and gave her a sad smile. "I don't know who it was that fucked over you so bad that you have to think all men are assholes, but some of us are really not all that bad. We made a deal. That deal bought my silence, not just from the cops, but from everybody. My best friend for over twenty years and I have no secrets from each other except one – you!"

She started to say something, but Jack was coming back so she just took a sip of her white wine. The rest of lunch was pleasant, even though I had a very hard time keeping my eyes off of Sandra. As we were leaving the restaurant Jack shook my hand, said he would review my bid and give me a call in a few days. I watched Sandra and Jack walk away and I just could not take my eyes off her until she was out of sight.

***

Two days later Jack called me and asked me to meet him for a drink at Mario's. I found him sitting in a corner booth and I joined him. As soon as the waitress had brought me my drink Jack said, "You were not the low bidder, but cost is not the only thing important to me. I prefer to do business with people that I trust and I trust you. You know why?"

Before I had a chance to ask he went on, "I trust you because

Sandra trusts you. You impressed her the day she hit you and not many men can do that to Sandra."

He saw the alarm show on my face and he smiled. "Yes, I know the whole story. Sandra and I have a rather unique relationship. I can't keep up with her in bed and so I let her seek whatever she needs as long as there are no secrets between us and she comes home to me. Sandra needed to avoid the police because she does not have a driver's license. She has been in front of the judge twice for driving without one and the last time he told her that if he saw her again, she was going to be his guest for sixty days.

I try to get her to take cabs, but she is a very headstrong woman. She believes that driving is a right and not a privilege and neither the judge nor I have been able to convince her otherwise. My calling you for a bid wasn't an accident. I didn't just pick up a phone book and pull your name out of it. Sandra took down your license plate number and I used some contacts to find out who you were. I'll fax you the signed contracts in the morning. Now if you will excuse me I have some place else I need to be."

I stood up, we shook hands and he left. I sat down and was taking a sip of my drink when a voice behind me said, "A man shouldn't have to drink alone. May I join you?"

I turned and saw Sandra standing there. I stood up and asked her to have a seat. She sat down and said, "I suspect that Jack has already filled you in on our relationship?"

I nodded a yes.

"I'm here for two reasons. One is that I always pay my debts and I seem to recall that we never finished our agreement. The second reason is just a bit touchier. Jack is marvelous in bed, but he can't give me as much sex as I need. I don't need herds of men to do what two good men can do, and I'm tired of using the shotgun approach to find my other lovers. I've decided that what I need is a steady boyfriend to help out Jack. Think you could handle sharing me with him?"

My smile gave her the answer to that one and she smiled back at me. "I'm dying to see your place, shall we go?"

End of the 6th Story

Faye's Anal Buddy

I was one of those men who had a great desire to watch his wife have sex with another man. I guess my situation was a little unique because I had seen it happen before I married her, and it had been the most exciting thing I had ever seen.

It happened several months before we were married. Faye had been having second thoughts about getting married and she instigated an argument so she would have a reason for breaking off the engagement. The real reason, as I found out from my cousin Barb (who is Faye's best friend), was that an old boyfriend had come back to town. Faye had been madly in love with the guy and then something happened, then they split and the guy left town. She got over him, met me and we had gotten engaged. Then three months before our wedding he came back; and I guess Faye wasn't as over the guy as she thought.

For a week my pride kept me from calling Faye, then one day I realized that I'd better get my head out of my ass and try to get her back. One night after work I swung by her parents' house and as I turned onto the street, I saw her on the front porch in a hot and heavy embrace with another guy and then they went into the house. It had been my intention to knock on the door and see if I couldn't talk to Faye, but I couldn't very well do it while some other guy was there, so I parked and settled in to see if I could wait him out. An hour went by but he didn't come out. Finally my curiosity got the better of me. I got out of the car, walked around to the side of the house and looked into the side window of the living room, expecting to see them necking on the couch, but they weren't there. The next window I came to was Faye's bedroom and the shades were up just enough for me to see inside – and what I saw broke my heart. It had been dark and I hadn't gotten a good look at the guy when he was on the porch, but in the lighted room I got a good look – he was black as coal! Damn! My wife to be had been in love with a black man and I had never known.

Faye was on her knees with her head buried in a pillow and the guy was fucking her in her asshole. She had never let me have sex with her there even though I had asked her several times. I should have turned and walked away, but for some perverse reason I just had to stay there and punish myself. I stood there and watched as he finished in her ass, as she washed him off and then sucked his cock to get it hard again, and then I watched as she fucked him. I was angry, I was heartbroken, but I was also excited as hell at what I had seen, and I blew a load all over the vinyl siding before I turned and left to go and get on with my life.

Two weeks later there was a knock on my door and I opened it to find Faye standing there. "May I come in?" I stepped aside and when she was in, I closed the door behind her and followed her into the living room. She sat down on the couch while I sat down on the chair opposite and just looked at her. By that time I had gotten the story from my cousin and I had also seen her with the guy, so I just sat there and waited for her to tell me what she was doing there.

"How have you been?"

"Okay. I've been better, but I'm okay."

"Yeah, well – look Bobby, I'm sorry for what I did. I was nervous and unsure and well, hey, marriage is a big step and I was scared. But I've had time to think about it and I realized that I love you enough to want to try. Can we get back together?"

"For how long? Until another boyfriend comes back to town and you need to go and see if the spark is still there?"

"Oh, you know."

"Yeah Faye, I know. It's a small town; stuff gets around."

"I'm sorry. I was afraid of making a mistake. I loved you and I knew that I loved you, but I had loved him too and I had loved him for a lot longer than I had known you. I had to know if there was still anything there and I had to find out before I married you, not after."

"Is there?"

"No. Oh he was happy to see me, fed me a line of bullshit about how much he still loved me, how much he had missed me, but all he was looking for was a piece of ass. I knew after a couple of days that there wasn't anything left between us and that I'd screwed up big time when I broke it off with you."

The long and short of it was that we did get back together and the wedding went off on schedule.

Faye and I had been married just a little over a year when I asked her why she never would let me have anal sex with her.

"Because it hurts too bad."

"Didn't seem to bother you any when your ex-boyfriend did it to you."

"What do you mean?"

I told her what had happened the night I came over to try and talk to her.

"You stood there and watched?"

I nodded a yes.

"Oh Jesus. And that's why you never called and tried to talk to me?"

Again I nodded my head yes.

"Well if you watched you should have seen why he could and you can't."

"What's that mean?"

"His cock baby, didn't you see the size of his cock?"

"No, men's cocks are not something that I pay a whole of attention to."

"It's small, a little longer than yours, but not much bigger around than your thumb. He fits in my ass real nice, but you are too big honey, and it's a shame because I love anal sex. I just don't love it enough to suffer the pain I'd get from you."

I was quiet and just looked at her. She broke the silence. "How did you ever take me back after you saw that?"

"It's called love, Faye. Besides, it turned me on. I still get a hard on when I remember him pounding into your asshole."

"You can't be serious."

"Oh yes I am," and I pulled my hard cock out of my pants. "See?"

Later, as we relaxed and looked up at the ceiling, I thought that I'd take a shot. "Do you ever think about seeing him for anal sex?"

Faye lay there silent for a long time and then she said, "I've thought about it from time to time. In fact he even calls about once a month to try and talk me into sneaking away with him for a date."

"Have you?"

"Of course not!"

"Why not?"

"Because, silly, I love you and I could never cheat on you."

"It isn't cheating if I let you do it."

Faye rolled up on an elbow and looked down at my face, "What did you say?"

"I said it isn't cheating if I let you do it. It's only cheating if you are sneaking around behind my back."

"Are you telling me to have an affair with Andy?"

"No, I'm telling you that you can. Whether or not you do or don't is strictly up to you."

"Why are you telling me this?"

"Because I love you enough to want to see that you are happy. You love anal sex but can't get it from me, so go and get it from Andy. It's a win-win situation. I got turned on watching you get what you love. I'd like to see it again. We both win."

"I can't believe this. I can't believe that you would let another man fuck me."

I just shrugged and nothing more was said on the subject.

Two weeks went by and then one night I came home from work to find a very different Faye in the kitchen fixing dinner. She had a ton of make up on, was wearing five-inch heels, a very short mini skirt and an extremely low cut blouse. "Jesus Christ Faye, you look like a whore."

"Well baby, this is the way the Andy likes me to look; the sluttier the better."

"The way Andy likes you?"

"I'm trusting you on this honey. If you didn't mean what you said the other night, we had better turn off the lights, lock the doors and pretend we aren't home."

"What are you saying?"

"Andy called me today and I let him talk me into seeing him. I told him that you are out of town and he will be here at seven. What do you want me to do?"

"Fuck dinner. I guess I like you looking like a whore too." I pulled out my hard cock. "If you hurry you can suck me off and still have time to freshen your lipstick before he gets here."

***

I was in the closet when the doorbell rang and I heard his voice as he came in the door. "God, but don't you look like the whore you always were. Are you still as big a whore as you used to be?"

"Yes baby, you know I am."

"Are you my slut?"

"Oh god yes baby, I'm your slut and I've missed your cock so bad."

"Well then, get on your knees and put those slutty lips around my johnson."

For the next several minutes all I heard was a bunch of 'oh yeah's, 'god but I missed you's and finally, "Here it comes you cum drinking whore." Several minutes later a topless Faye led Andy into the bedroom by his cock and I saw what she meant. It was about nine inches long, but it wasn't a whole lot bigger around than a skinny hotdog.

"Okay my little whore, you know what I want first."

Faye stepped out of her skirt and bent forward over the bed. Her head was on the bed and she looked toward the closet, "Come on baby, do my ass. You know I love your cock in my ass and it's been so long since I've had it. Come on baby, come on and fuck me hard."

"Yeah, you are a fucking slut, aren't you."

"You know I am baby. Come on put it in, don't tease me, I need it baby, I need it."

He spit on his hand and stroked himself a couple of times and then he started to slide his cock in Faye's ass. I saw her wince when it first went in, but the her face relaxed and in a minute or so I heard her making sounds that I'd never heard her make before. "Oh god, oh sweet Jesus baby, that's it, that's it. Fuck me baby, fuck me. I've missed you baby, I've missed what you can do to me." She started squealing and her body shook; and then she gave a loud wail that sounded like "Oh god yes fuck my ass" and then a loud scream as she had a larger and longer orgasm than I had ever seen her have before.

Andy was poking her hard now and Faye was squealing like a pig when Andy said, "Here it comes, here it comes, here it comes you fucking whore."

It had been my idea to do it and my cock was harder than it had ever been before from watching it – but I was pissed. Faye had never been that turned on and vocal with me. Andy finished in her ass and then she went and got a wash rag and washed off his dick before going down on him again. When he was as hard as he wanted to be, he pulled her up, pushed her down on the bed and fucked her. Faye had warned me that Andy had to have his ego stroked and not to get mad at what I heard her say, but even forewarned it still came as a shock to listen to her.

"Skinny white boy can't take care of your ass, that's why you had to call on the Hammer, right?"

"Yes baby, yes. Nobody has ever fucked me as good as you do."

"Tell me what you want baby."

"I want your cock baby, I want your wonderful cock."

"You want this black sausage in your ass again?"

"Oh God yes baby, my ass is yours whenever you want it. I love your big black cock stuffed in my ass."

"That honky fuck you married can't satisfy you can he?"

"No baby, he can't. Nobody can satisfy me like you do."

"Tell me what you want."

"You baby, I want you."

"That isn't what I want to hear, you fucking slut."

"I want your cock baby."

"Tell me what you are."

"I'm a whore baby, I'm your whore."

"That's not what I want to hear, slut. Say it."

"I'm your whore baby, I'm a whore for nigger cock."

"Say it!"

"Fuck me nigger, fuck your nigger loving white trash whore."

"You are the only white that can say that to me and not get hurt, but as long as you give me your ass I'll be what?"

"My nigger baby, my nigger cock."

"Oh god but I do like fucking married white sluts."

"I'm yours baby. I'm yours for as long as you want to feed me that cock of yours."

When I thought about what it would be like to watch from the closet, I was thinking along the lines of maybe an hour or so and Andy would be gone. But this fucking guy was like the Energizer Bunny – he just kept going and going and going. He fucked Faye four times in her pussy, twice in her ass and she sucked his cock to completion twice, and that's not counting the blow job he got when he walked in the front door. And all the time it was talk, talk, talk. I was in that fucking closet for over three and a half-hours and he still wanted more. "Come on baby, let me stay the night. You haven't gotten my balls empty yet."

"I can't Andy. I want to but I can't take a chance. If anyone saw you come in tonight I can always tell Bobby that an old friend stopped by. If they see you leave in the morning, he would know I'm cheating on him."

"That's okay baby, you could come live with me and I could spend all my time buried in your sweet ass."

"Sorry baby, you know I love your beautiful black cock, but I love my husband too."

"When can we do this again?"

"I don't know baby. I only said yes for tonight because Bobby is out of town and he doesn't do that very often."

"He bowl or go to lodge meetings or anything like that?"

"No, he doesn't."

"Work on it baby, find him something to do to keep his white ass busy. I just love to take a white man's pussy and fuck it. Get me back here baby. Oh, hot damn, look at what happened while we were talking. Where do you want it baby?"

Faye glanced over at the closet and said, "In my ass lover, in my ass," and she turned and bent over the bed, spread her legs and grabbed the mattress.

I came out of the closet as soon as the two of them were out of the room and I stripped and waited for Faye to return. I'd jacked off three times in the closet and I was still as hard as an iron bar. I sure hoped that Faye was ready for at least one more fuck because she was going to get it, ready or not. Five minutes went by and still no Faye, so I tiptoed out of the bedroom and down the hall and then peeked around the corner to the living room. Faye was on her knees giving him another blow job! Shit, the way things were going, he might even fuck her again. Well, if he was going to and they wanted the bed instead of the living room couch or the floor, he was going to find the "white honky" on the bed because I wasn't going back into that closet.

It was another ten minutes before Faye came back to the room. I was lying on the bed stroking my cock and she stopped in the doorway, looked at me and said, "Does that mean that you are still talking to me?"

"Why wouldn't we be talking?"

"You've never seen before what a slut I can be."

"Just out of curiosity: did he nail you again?"

"Twice. A blow job and a fuck on the living room floor."

"How many more times would he have gone if he had spent the night?"

"Maybe five or six more times."

"Why in God's name did you ever come back to me? You loved it! I've never gotten you to be that way. I know you warned me that most of what you would say would be bullshit, but I know that you meant a lot of it."

"Did you see any love there, baby? Did you see any affection, any tenderness? All that was there was the sex. And yes I loved it, especially the anal, but I need more than that. I need what I get from you baby, I need the love you give me."

"Does your pussy have room for another cock tonight?"

"You really want to stick your lily white cock into a black man's whore? You really want a nigger's left overs? I don't know white boy, what's in it for me?"

"You treat me right and I just might take up bowling or join a lodge or something."

"You think you could handle it on a regular basis?"

"Why don't you come over here and handle this and then maybe we can talk about it."

Faye and I did talk about it the next morning and the bottom line was that she would like to keep seeing Andy, but only if I was sure that I could handle it. For the next month Faye saw Andy twice a week on my "bowling nights." Sometimes I was in the closet and sometimes I did actually go out and find something to do. As much as I liked watching Faye be Andy's whore and as turned on as it made me, there are only so many times that you can stand in a closet for three and four hours. Either way, coming out of the closet or coming home after, I would attack Faye and fuck her until I couldn't get it up anymore.

Then one day I came home from work horny as a goat and Faye begged off. "Please baby, not tonight. I don't feel well." That was a first. In our entire married life, Faye had never said no to me. I didn't think anything of it because we all don't feel well from time to time, but when it happened the next two nights, I asked her if maybe she should go see a doctor. She told me no, that she was starting to get over it. The next night was a night when Andy would be coming over, and I suggested that she call him and cancel. "No, I'll be okay by then. Besides, I've said no to you for three days now and I want you coming out of that closet loaded for bear."

"I won't be in the closet tomorrow. I'm playing cards with some of the guys from work."

"No, you have to be there tomorrow. Please honey, I need you to be there."

I was settled into the closet when the doorbell rang. "How's my little white whore tonight?"

"I'm ready for you baby. All three holes are just aching for big, black cock."

"Hear that boys? The white slut wants all of you."

Several voices said "oh yeah" and "can't wait." What the fuck was going on? The answer came soon enough – Faye came walking through the bedroom door followed by Andy and five other black men. With a quick nervous glance at the closet, she dropped her skirt and said, "Okay, who goes first this time?"

For the next four hours the six black men fucked Faye in every hole that she had. They took her two at a time, three at a time and once she had a cock in her mouth, one in her ass and one in her pussy while two guys held her upright so she could jack off a guy standing next to the bed. She screamed, begged, and pleaded for more cock, for them to fuck her harder and faster, for them to cum in her, for them to feed her more big, black cock and for them to make her their slut. When the last man finished and Andy was walking out the bedroom door, he looked down at her on the bed and said, "See you tomorrow slut. Be ready for me and my boys."

She was on the bed, head buried in a pillow, ass up in the air when I came out of the closet. She didn't look at me. She just said, "Take my ass. Please don't say anything, just take my ass. They opened it up for you. Please baby, take my ass at least once before you throw me out."

I looked at her ass and saw that they had indeed opened it up. It was so open that I could have pushed my hand in it. My cock, which had been rock hard when I came out of the closet, wilted and I walked out of the room. I now knew why Faye had begged off having sex with me for the last three days. Andy's "see you tomorrow" had said it all. He wasn't just fucking her a couple of nights a week, he was also coming over during the day and from the way Faye said "Who is first this time," I knew that he hadn't been coming alone. Faye didn't have the nerve to tell me, so she wanted me in the closet so I could find out the hard way. I could hear her sobbing in the bedroom as I sat on the couch staring at the wall and asking myself what had I done to us.

End of the 7th Story

———✃———

Stopping To See Eve

It was my least favorite day of the week. It was the day after payday and the day I had to stop by my ex-wife's place and hand her the child support and alimony check. I didn't begrudge the kids their child support, but it just killed me to pay Eve alimony. Especially since the divorce was caused by her and what she did; or more to the point, didn't do.

***

I had gone through a bitter divorce and when it was final, I swore off women. They were treacherous and unfaithful whores – all of them – and I was staying away from all of them from then on. It went all the way back to high school. I went steady with Brenda for nine months and all she would let me do was play with her tits and do some heavy necking. She kept telling me that she wasn't 'that kind of a girl' but I guess what she meant was that she wasn't that kind of a girl *with me.* One night when I was supposed to be at a family function with my folks, I swung by her house and found her pulling a train for some guys on the football team.

Next was Darby who told me that she loved me to death and kept trying to get me to propose to her even though (as I came to find out) she had a steady date every Wednesday with two guys whose cocks she sucked. Then it was off to college where Bethany, Mary and Millie all proved to be faithless sluts.

Then I met Angel, and everything seemed to be magical between us, and I proposed and she accepted. Two days before the wedding a guy I knew said:

"You aren't really serious about marrying Angel, are you?"

"Of course I am. Why shouldn't I be?"

"Are you one of those guys who gets off on his girl fucking other guys?"

"Hell no."

"Then you better stay away from Angel."

"Why? What do you know?"

"At her bridal shower the other girls brought in a stripper, and when he finished dancing, Angel sucked him off and then he fucked her while the other girls cheered them on. When it was done she gave him her phone number and asked him to call. He did and she has seen him three times since the night of the party."

"How could you know that?"

"I was the stripper."

That night I told Angel what I'd found out, asked her if it was true and she ran crying into the bathroom, locked the door and wouldn't come out. I could hear her crying and saying over and over:

"I'm sorry, I'm sorry, I'm sorry. I didn't mean to, I'm sorry."

I packed up and moved out of the apartment we shared. I graduated, found a job and decided to stay away from women. That decision lasted all of a month and then I met Jennifer. We clicked and after our fourth date we started having sex. After six months Jenn asked me if I'd given any thought to marriage and I told her bluntly that I hadn't. She asked me why and I told her the whole sad story, and added that I just couldn't bring myself to trust women any more.

"That's silly, baby. So you had a run of bad luck with some girls, so what? Not all women are easy sluts. I love you baby and I could never do something like that to the man I love."

Jenn kept after me to get married and finally, after almost a year, I caved in and married her. The marriage hummed along and it certainly seemed that Jenn was right when she said I'd just had a run of bad luck with the wrong girls. Then one afternoon in the third year of our marriage, I came early to find her on her knees in the living room giving some guy I'd never seen before a blow job. I proceeded to beat the snot out of the asshole, and while I was doing that, Jennifer got on the phone, called the cops, told them that I was on a rampage and that she feared for her safety. The cops were there in minutes, pulled me off of the asshole that I'd caught with my wife and took me off to jail.

When it was over and the divorce was final I said, "Fuck all women" and got on with my life. When I needed or wanted sex, I used professionals; it was just so much easier that way.

***

The thing about being a dedicated bachelor is that no one can stand it. The married women you know seem to take it as a personal affront to them and they are forever trying to fix you up with some candidate "Who is just perfect for you" and who will end your bachelor status. The married men that you know do the same, only their reason is that they can't stand to see you happy when they aren't. The solution? Drag you down into the pit with them. I soon got to the point where I automatically found excuses every time someone invited me over for dinner or to a party.

But there is always someone that you can't say no to and one of those someone's was my best friend Tom. Tom asked me over for a barbecue one Saturday and when I got there, I found that there were four couples and a single woman. Not again, I thought, but Tom was my best friend so I didn't turn and bolt for the door. What I did do, after Tom's wife Mary Beth introduced me to Eve, was ignore her. It wasn't an easy thing to do. Eve was a tall woman – about five foot nine – with a trim figure, long red hair and the face of an angel; but all of the other women in my life had been great looking also. That was probably one of the reasons they were so popular with other guys. Mary Beth would have had better luck trying to set me up with an ugly woman.

I spent all my time at the party socializing with the others who were there. Half way through the party, Mary Beth came up to me and asked me why I was behaving 'so crassly' toward Eve.

"I'm not behaving anything toward her. I don't know her and I don't want to know her."

"Still, she is alone and it wouldn't hurt you any to be a little more social where she is concerned."

"And just why is she here alone, Mary Beth? You and I both know the answer to that question. You invited the both of us with the intent on getting us together even when knowing how I feel about that. If she is not having a good time, Mary Beth, it is your fault, not mine. If you felt the need to fix her up with someone, you should have picked someone other than me."

She gave me a nasty look and went storming off. A couple of minutes later Tom came up to me:

"Sorry bud. I warned her, but she just knew the two of you would be right for each other."

"How so?"

"Eve has been married twice and both marriages ended when she caught her husbands with other women. Mary Beth was sure that you would be comfortable with a woman who felt that way about cheating. I mean, just how likely is it that a woman like that would cheat on her man? Mary Beth convinced Eve that someone who has been through what you have wouldn't be likely to cheat on his woman. Mary Beth thought that it would be a match made in Heaven."

"Yeah, well, I'm sorry Tom, but you know that I've sworn off women and I'm not about to change my mind."

Shortly after talking with Mary Beth and Tom, I left and went home.

***

I was extremely surprised when two days later I received a call at work from Eve. She was going to be near where I worked at lunchtime and she asked me to have lunch with her. My first impulse was to say that I was sorry, that I was snowed under with work and couldn't get away from my desk. At the same time I was intrigued: why was a woman I ignored calling me? I agreed to meet her at a restaurant across the street from my office building. She cut right to the chase:

"I'm a pretty good looking broad and I'm not all that used to men ignoring me. The fact that you did arouse my curiosity and being a rather forward type of individual, I decided to go to the source to find out why."

"The fact of the matter is that it had nothing to do with you. My behavior that day was aimed at Mary Beth. I wanted to make her as uncomfortable as I could where you were concerned. I'd had it up to my eyebrows with her constant attempts to fix me up with someone. I'd told her at least fifty times not to do it, that I didn't want it, and she still went and did it anyway. I figured that if I ignored whoever she invited to meet me, it might embarrass her enough to make her stop."

"Mary Beth told me your past circumstances and I can't say I blame you for not wanting a woman prowling around the edges of your life, but you do know that we all aren't bitches, don't you?"

To make a long story a little shorter, by the end of lunch I had asked her out and nine months later we were married.

***

The first two years were great and then the first kid came along and Eve transferred all of her attention to little Jenny. I'm not saying that Eve split her attention between Jenny and me; I'm saying that I got *no* attention and Jenny got it all. Our sex life went from three and four times a week before Jenny (right up to the eighth month) to once every two weeks after Jenny. With me getting so little sex, it was amazing that Eve managed to get pregnant again, but it happened. After Jimmy was born Eve had no time for me at all. Everything was Jenny this and Jimmy that. Sex went to once a month and then to once every six weeks. All I was around the house was the breadwinner and not even a good one, according to Eve, who always seemed to need money for something.

I made the unilateral decision to get a vasectomy as I sure wasn't going to father another kid and make it even worse than it already was. This outraged Eve because she had her heart set on having four kids. I responded with:

"You need to have sex to get pregnant and we don't, remember?"

"Is that all you think about is sex?"

"It is when I don't get any." And things went downhill from there.

I began working late, meeting fellow workers after work for a beer – anything to keep from going home – and then one night I came home and Eve and the kids weren't there. There was a note on the kitchen table telling me that she had gone to spend a few days visiting her mother. The next morning as I left the house for work, a man came up to me and served me with divorce papers. Eve was claiming "irreconcilable differences." Well, I'd always known women were treacherous bitches. I didn't bother to fight the divorce except to point out that the house was mine before we got married. Why bother, we didn't have a *marriage* anyway.

***

Six months after the divorce, Eve moved in with a guy and they set up housekeeping. Didn't get married, just moved in together. I know in my heart that the reason Eve didn't marry the guy was so she could still gouge me for alimony. Nine months after they moved in together, Eve had her third kid and eleven months later she had her fourth.

In our city, the Friend of the Court was notoriously inefficient and the child support and alimony payments sent to them could take up to six weeks to get to those who they were intended for. After several calls from Eve telling me that she had no money to buy food for the kids, I got into the habit of hand-carrying the checks to her. I made the check out to her and down in the left hand corner on the line that said "For" I put in 'child support and alimony payment for (and the date) and I'd have Eve initial it. If I ever got called in for non-support, I would be covered.

I usually timed my visits so I could spend an hour or so with Jenny and Jimmy before I left. On this particular night I was running late and when I got there Eve had already put the kids to bed. With the kids in bed I had no reason to stay, so I gave Eve the check, waited for her to initial it and I had turned to go when Eve said:

"Wait a second Art, I have something I need to talk with you about. Please sit down on the couch and I'll be right back."

She left the room and three minutes later she came back in the room stark naked except for a pair of high heels. I have to admit that I got an immediate hard on.

"What the hell is this about Eve?"

"It's what I need to talk with you about Art. Herb isn't worth a shit in bed and I'm going crazy. I need a good fuck, Art. Herb is working swings this month so we have five hours before he will get home. Help me out here Art, please?"

"What the fuck is wrong with you Eve? One of the reasons for the divorce was that you *wouldn't* fuck me."

"That's ancient history Art. I'm offering now. No strings attached pussy. I don't know what went wrong in our marriage, but you were always great in bed. Help me out here Art, please?"

Talk about mixed emotions – I had a bunch of them. As many times as I had been cheated on, it went against the grain for me to do to some other guy what had been done so often to me. But I had an immense dislike of Herb because he was living off *my* money. I knew for a fact that my alimony check paid the rent, and that his paycheck covered groceries and utilities and had enough left over to pay for them to go out and party every weekend. The bastard wouldn't make Eve marry him; he just coasted along on my money.

Then there was Eve herself. I had spent the better part of the last three years wishing for all kinds of bad things to happen to her, so why should I help her out? On the other hand, I hadn't been laid in almost a month and on the weekend I had intended to call a friend of a friend who was a light hook. I could do Eve, save myself some money and get back at Herb all at the same time. While all that roiled around in my head, I had an idea. That little light bulb you see in cartoons came on just over my head. Why not, I said to myself. Do her and do her so good that she will want to do it again the next time I stopped by. I stood up and said:

"You want it, you come and get it," and I stood there to see what she would do.

She stood there looking at me for a second and then her tongue licked her lips and she walked toward me. When she got to me she said, "You do the shirt and I'll get the rest."

She knelt down in front of me and undid my belt. Next she pulled my zipper down and undid the top button of my trousers and pulled them down. I kicked my loafers off and then stepped out of the trousers that had pooled around my ankles. My erection had tented my boxers and Eve reached out and ran her fingers over it as I tossed my shirt and undershirt on the floor. Eve looked up at me with an unreadable expression on her face and then she pulled my boxers down. My cock, suddenly freed from constraint, bobbed up and down and Eve leaned forward and captured it with her mouth. I lifted my feet so Eve could get my boxers out of the way and she tossed them to the side.

Eve pulled back and took her mouth off me and looked at my cock and then she took me back in. Her hands came up to my ass cheeks and she pulled me forward until my cock was deep in her throat and then started to work on me. She had always given marvelous head except she would never swallow. She would let me cum in her mouth, but then she would spit it out into a Kleenex. Not this time, I thought, oh no, not this time.

I stood there looking down at Eve sucking my cock and planned how I was going to get even with her for what she had done. When I felt myself getting ready to shoot, I grabbed Eve's head with both hands and held on tight as I shoved my cock into her mouth as far as it would go and let my juice blast the back of her throat. She tried to pull back, but I wasn't going to let her. She had no choice; she had to swallow or choke. I held her head until my cock went limp and then I took my hands away and let them fall to my sides. Eve jerked her head back and looked up at me with angry eyes and spat out:

"You bastard! You know I hate that."

"I'm not your husband any more Eve and I don't have to worry about what you like and don't like. The only one I have to worry about is me and that was what I wanted to do. Now, are you going to get me hard again or should I get dressed and leave?"

"You don't have to be an asshole Art," she said as she took my limp cock in her hand and lifted it to her mouth.

You ain't seen nothing yet lady, I thought to myself. While she worked on getting me hard again, I thought back to the first time I had seen her. What was it Tom had said to me? Something about how she would never cheat because she knew what it felt like to be cheated on? Maybe Herb didn't count since they weren't married.

Eve had me up in minutes and I pulled her up and led her over to the couch. I picked my T-shirt up off the floor and handed it to her.

"What am I supposed to do with this?" she asked.

"Wad it up and put it in your mouth. You always were a screamer and we don't want to wake up the kids."

"Oh Art, ever the romantic," she said as I worked a finger into her pussy. I started finger-fucking her to get some moisture flowing and she said, "You could get the same result, and maybe even faster, if you were to go down on me. Herb won't do it for me and you know how much I love it."

"Maybe I could, but I don't trust you Eve. For all I know the asshole ripped off a piece before going to work. I wouldn't put it past you to try and get me to go down on you, lick up his dick snot and make me believe that it is just *your* natural wetness."

"Oh come on Art, you can't really believe that I would do something like that to you."

"Given everything else you've done to me, I'd almost bet on it."

I saw what I took to be a momentary glint of evil in her eyes and I would bet that I had just primed the pump. She would ask me back, fuck Herb just before he left for work and then she would do her best to try and get me to eat her pussy. I don't know how she thought she could con me into it, but I had no doubt she was already planning it in her mind.

My fingers had loosened her up a little and then I moved her legs apart and got between them. I rubbed the head of my dick up and down the folds of her pussy and she moaned and said, "Put it in honey. Please don't tease me; put it in and fuck me."

I lined my cock up and pushed. She could have been a little wetter, but what the hell, her comfort wasn't all that high on my list of things that needed to be. I started driving into her and in about four strokes I was all the way in, pubic bone to pubic bone, and then I started to fuck her hard. I slammed into her, bam bam bam, and after about two minutes she moaned out a string, "Oh yes, oh yes oh yes, oh yes," and then the string changed to a low, keening wail that I knew from experience would soon change into a scream. I grabbed my T-shirt, stuffed it into her mouth and then I fucked her as hard and fast as I could. She arched her body and pushed her hips up at me, her nails clawed at my back and her heels were drumming on the backs of my legs. I was pounding hard and I felt the build-up and then I blew my load as deep into her as I could.

I held myself in her until my cock was soft and then I pulled out and stood up. Eve looked up at me and said, "God, but did I ever need that. Again? You have time to do it again?"

It turned out that I had time to do it two more times before Eve told me that I had to leave before Herb got home. She walked me to the door and just before I opened it, she threw her arms around me and gave me a passionate kiss. She broke the kiss and stepped back and asked, "Can you stop by at the same time the next time you come over?"

"Yeah Eve, I can do that," I said and as I was going down the front steps, I had a big smile on my face – and it wasn't because I'd just gotten laid.

***

The following Friday, I arrived at Eve's about half an hour after the kids had gone to bed and Eve answered the door in a lacy black see-through robe and high heels. She threw her arms around me as soon as I was in the door and gave me a passionate kiss. She broke the kiss and her hands went to my zipper, but I grabbed them and stopped her.

"Do me a favor and go up and make sure the kids are asleep."

"They are. I looked in on them just before you got here."

"Humor me, okay?"

She went up the stairs and as soon as she turned the corner to go down the hall, I opened the front door and let Jimmy in. He was carrying his video camera and I had him duck into the hall closet. A minute or so later, Eve came down and told me that the kids were all sound asleep. She took me by the hand and led me over to the couch and had me sit down. She unzipped me and proceeded to give me one of her superior blow jobs. She licked and sucked on me until I came; and that time she swallowed it without any fuss at all and I knew what that meant: she *had* fucked Herb just before he left the house and now she was going to try and get me to go down on her. How could I refuse when she swallowed all I had with no protest? When I was limp, she stood up and dropped the robe.

"I haven't had sex with Herb in three days honey. I'm clean down there. Would you eat my pussy, please honey, please?"

The lying bitch! I had known from the last time that she was going to try and get me to eat her while Herb's juices were still in her. Doing it was going to be distasteful, but it would be a small price to pay for what I was going to do to her, so I said:

"Okay. Let's do it sixty-nine," and I undressed and laid down on the couch so she would be on top and facing away from the front door. I knew Jimmy had the closet door open a crack and was taping everything Eve and I were doing, but I wanted Eve facing the other way so Jimmy could come out, move off to the side and get better footage.

As soon as my tongue slipped between the folds of her pussy, I knew that I had been right. I'd eaten her a hundred times when we were married and I knew full well that her normal taste was nowhere near the salty taste I was getting. No matter, just one more reason for not feeling bad about what I was going to do to her. Let her think she was putting something over on me; it would keep her attention off from what was going on around her.

After several minutes she had me hard again and I got her on her hands and knees, still facing away from the door, and I took her doggie style. I took it slow and easy until she started moaning and hissing, "Oh god, oh god, oh god, oh yes, oh yes," and then I picked up the pace. Jimmy was off to the side where Eve couldn't see him shooting the action. I made a hand sign and, as pre-arranged, he set down the camera and undressed. I started slamming my cock into Eve as hard as I could and the keening wail started and began building toward the scream. She bit down on one of the couch pillows and her body shuddered as her orgasm grabbed her. At just that moment I pulled out of Eve and stepped back; Jimmy took my place and started slamming his cock into her as I picked up the camera and recorded the action. The hope was that Eve wouldn't notice the quick change, but even if she did we didn't intend to stop.

Jimmy kept pounding her and I got some excellent footage of his coal black cock driving into Eve's white body. Eve still hadn't noticed that it wasn't me fucking her. I set the camera down and moved quietly to the front door and Sam, Todd and Ralph quietly came in, moved off to the side and undressed. Sam picked up the camera and began shooting as I moved to the head of the couch.

The first Eve knew that I wasn't fucking her came when I reached down, grabbed her head with both hands and lifted it up. I saw confusion and then awareness, but whatever she was going to say when she opened her mouth was lost when I shoved my cock into her open hole. I fucked her face while Jimmy pounded her cunt and Sam taped it all. Jimmy raised his hand, the signal that he was cumming, and Ralph moved up to take his place. The switch took place with the smoothness of a baton pass in a relay race. I had been close to getting off when I switched with Jimmy, so it wasn't long before I raised my hand and Todd moved up. As soon as I sent my load down Eve's throat, I moved away and Todd moved right in.

I went and relieved Sam as the cameraman and he moved over closer to the action, ready to get his wick wet. The first thing I noticed when I put my eye to the viewfinder was that Eve was pushing her ass back at Ralph as he drove into her. Eve was quite a sight with a black cock at each end of her and I panned the room to show the other two black men. As far as I knew, Eve wasn't a racist, but Herb sure was and he was going to love the living hell out of the video I was planning on giving him.

By the time I had that thought, Todd had taken his hands from Eve's head to see what she would do and she didn't try to pull her head away from him. She was sucking cock on her own and after that, it was the five of us taking turns on Eve. We never gave her a break. As soon as one was out, another was in. I looked at the clock and saw that I had time for one more, so I told the guys that when they got their rocks off, they needed to get dressed and out of the house before Herb got home. When Jimmy came in her cunt and moved out of the way, I took his place and drove my cock into her swamp of a pussy. I stroked into her cunt half a dozen times to get my dick wet and then I did something that she had never let me do – I took her ass!

She squealed and tried to get away, but Ralph and Sam held her in place. I was gentle, I went slowly, but I did take her ass. Once I began stroking into her butt the guys let go of her and dressed and one by one left until only Jimmy was there shooting me fucking Eve's ass. When he had a couple of minutes of it he waved at me and he left too. I didn't care if Herb caught me or not; I was going to finish in Eve's ass.

For the first time that night, Eve didn't have a cock in her mouth and she was free to express herself:

"You bastard!" she snarled, "You rotten mother fucking bastard!"

I smiled as I kept pounding into her butt. She was cussing me, but she was also pushing her ass back at me, so I thought I would check something out. I stopped pushing into her and pulled my cock out of her ass.

"Don't you dare!" she cried, "Don't you fucking dare. You started this and you have to finish it."

I laughed as I slid my dick back into her and started fucking her hard. It took a couple more minutes, but then I came, pulled out and started gathering my clothes. Eve was still on the couch with her head on a pillow and her ass in the air. I finished dressing and I said:

"Same time next week?"

"Get out of here you rotten bastard, get out, get out, get out!" she yelled at me and I laughed as I left the house.

***

I made several copies of the tape, meaning to give one copy to Herb and then mail the rest to family and friends, but I never did. I ended up keeping the original for myself and destroyed the rest. I owed Eve for what she had done to me, but when push came to a shove, I couldn't bring myself to be that big of an asshole. I still hand deliver the check to Eve but I never go over there after the kids have gone to bed., And once I'm there Eve leaves the room and doesn't come back until I'm gone. I wonder what she's thinking. Does she wish I would come later? Would she want me to come alone if I did? Or would she have a gun ready and shoot me as soon as I walked in the door? I'll never know, because it just isn't going to happen.

End of the 8th Story

Ruby's Medical Problem

My story was like a thousand others – a hundred thousand others – and it took place every day of the week: get up in the morning, my lovely wife of twelve years would fix my breakfast, wish me a good day at work, kiss me goodbye and send me on my way; go to work, put in my eight to ten hours and then head home to the loving wife who had dinner ready and on the table. After dinner, we sit on the couch and watch TV while holding hands or read until bedtime and then we go upstairs and make mad, passionate love. I would fall asleep thinking how lucky I was to have a job I liked, a woman I loved, and a woman who loved me.

Ruby and I met in college, fell in love and went steady for three years before getting married right after graduation. I wasn't Ruby's first nor was she mine, so our first lovemaking wasn't a series of mistakes. We both knew what we wanted from each other and we were not at all hesitant in letting each other know where to push, where to touch, where to stroke; and the result was a sexual nirvana the like of which I had never experienced before. I looked forward to spending the rest of my life with this beautiful, sexually exciting woman.

Our road to the wedding chapel was not an easy one. We were both strong-minded and some of our disagreements were very heated – some to the point of causing us to break up. Ruby always found another boyfriend and seemed to go out of her way to rub my nose in the fact that she was letting someone else have her body; but somehow we always managed to end up back together. I didn't go looking for anyone during these separations because, like most guys on a full ride football scholarship, I just didn't have a whole lot of free time once practice and the season started. That's not to say that I didn't occasionally have something just drop into my lap.

Once, at a frat party, I came downstairs after a very spirited romp with a gorgeous redhead to find Ruby, on the arm of her current lover, giving me a withering look. A couple of months later, when we were back together, she made some catty remark about "that redheaded slut that was hanging all over you," seemingly oblivious to the fact that at the time, she was fucking the guy she was with when she saw me and Sally. I found it to be humorous and I smiled and got a "What's so god damned funny" for my trouble.

Whatever, we made it through college, learned not to argue with each other and got married. The next twelve years went quickly by. I found a job that I liked, was good at, and that paid well. Ruby, who had majored in Computer Science, got involved with a dot.com start up and was one of the smart ones who got out before the big bust and she'd made enough money that neither one of us had to work again. But I liked my job and everyone needs to be doing something, right? Ruby started a consulting business and worked out of our house. We bought several time-shares: a week in Vail, a week in Ft. Lauderdale and a week in Palm Springs. Our weekends were spent flying to places we had never been and then flying back home. Life was one big adventure for us, and as a result our marriage never reached the 'stale' stage where so many other marriages seemed to fall prey to.

Ruby refused to let our love life go stale. She was inventive and always wanted to try out something new and her appetite for sex was enormous. There were many nights I would come home from work and have Ruby tell me she wanted a 'quickie' before dinner, and then we would never get out of the bedroom. She was the perfect wife, loving, caring and a sexual dynamo. I worked hard to keep up with her and I do mean I had to work hard. In high school and college, I was constantly in training for one sport or another and as a result I had been in great shape.

Following graduation from college, the sudden cessation of daily physical training (combined with the good life I was now leading) tended to put some poundage where it wasn't wanted or needed. Ruby had made the comment one day that she hoped I wouldn't get so out of shape that she would have to take a lover or two to help me fill my husbandly obligations. Some time in front of a full-length mirror and an honest self-appraisal convinced me that I needed to get back on a full regime of exercise. It took me six months, but I got back to my college playing weight and daily exercise was keeping me there. Ruby of course commented on it, "Greedy bastard aren't you. Want to keep me all to yourself I suppose. I was so looking forward to getting you some help. Oh well, maybe you will fall off the wagon. Come on lover, let's go and put those muscles to good use."

So, good job, good physical shape, great wife, great love life, and a great marriage – life was good!

***

Right up to the day I came home early and found out that Ruby had indeed gone and gotten me some help. I'd come home early because I'd just finished a project that had made my company a bundle of money, and my boss had given me the rest of the week off as an added bonus. I got home and found two strange cars parked in the driveway, and so I had to park in the street. When I walked in the front door, I immediately knew what was going on because I could hear it all the way down stairs; one long wail that I knew only too well, "Giveittome giveittome giveittome don't stop damn you giveittome."

I debated turning around and walking out, but realized that it would only eat at me until I got back home. If I walked upstairs right then, I'd at least have the satisfaction of ruining someone else's day. But I didn't do that either. I hollered up the stairs as loud as I could, "Honey, I'm home. I'll make a pitcher of martinis and be right up."

Then I went into the kitchen and did just that. The kitchen is so situated that you can see the stair way and I saw two guys in their twenties rushing down the stairs trying to get dressed while trying to get out. I almost laughed, but didn't. I took the pitcher of martinis and two glasses and climbed the stairs to face the trembling, guilt-ridden wife who would beg me for forgiveness – but she wasn't there that day. What I found was a slightly bemused Ruby, legs still spread, pussy lips still a bit puffy from the recent workout that I had interrupted. She greeted me with, "Well, you sure know how to ruin a girls day."

I looked at her and said, "You and your two friends haven't done a whole lot for mine."

I poured her a martini and then took mine and went over and sat in the chair across from the bed. She sipped her drink and watched me, absolutely no remorse showing. I could not believe how calmly I was taking this, at least outwardly – inside my guts were churning – and I said, "Where do we go from here?"

You could have knocked me over with a feather when the brazen bitch said, "Well for starters you could get over here and finish what Hal and Phil started. I was right on the edge of cumming when you terrified the poor dears."

I was so surprised that I actually started to get up and do it, but then caught myself and sat back down. Ruby giggled and said, "Don't fight it, lover. Right now you are looking at me, lying here freshly fucked, and you want me. Your face might be saying 'bullshit' but the tent in your trousers is saying otherwise. You know you won't be able to think straight while half the blood you need to make your brain operate is in the head of your cock. You might as well take care of it now. You'll feel better and then we can talk".

I sat in the chair with my jaw hanging open. I finally got myself under control and took a sip of my martini. "How can you even think that I would want to follow someone else into your unfaithful cunt?"

Ruby grinned at me. "It shouldn't bother you at all, lover. You have been doing it for years and it hasn't slowed you down any."

I sat in my chair and thought to myself that this wasn't real, that I must be asleep and having a nightmare. In real life I'd be raging, throwing chairs, punching my fist into the wall and screaming at Ruby. She would be crying, cowering at my rage, begging forgiveness and making promises that it would never happen again. I shook my head to clear it and said, "How long has this been going on?"

Ruby looked me straight in the eye and said, "How long have we known each other?"

I looked at her with disbelief written all over my face and she said, "That's right baby. I've had lovers on the side since the day I met you. The only time I wasn't getting some extra cock was on our honeymoon."

I stood up and started to leave the room. "Where are you going?" I didn't answer, and as I got to the head of the stairs she cried, "David come back here, I need you."

I turned and went back to the bedroom door. She was off the bed and pulling on a robe. "You don't need me Ruby. I don't know what you do need, but it obviously never was me," and I left the house.

I spent the night in a motel with my cell phone turned off and having the rest of the week off. Then I drove back to the neighborhood and parked down the street from the house. My pager started going off about nine which was what time the switchboard at the office opened. I surmised that Ruby was trying to reach me at the office and that they in turn were trying to get a message to me. I turned my cell phone on and it started ringing almost immediately and the caller ID showed that it was Ruby. I ignored the cell phone and the pager and around ten-thirty I saw Ruby back out of the garage and head toward town.

I went into the house, grabbed all my clothes, and cleaned out my home office. At the last minute I remembered my golf clubs and got them. I was certainly going to have plenty of time to play from now on. I drove back to the motel and checked back in for a couple of more days and then I called the office. There were nineteen messages from Ruby, and the receptionist told me to hold for Charlie, my boss. He came on the line and asked me where I was and I told him.

"Ruby is calling here every ten minutes. She's frantic to find you. You need to call her and let her know where you are, if for no other reason than to clear the switchboard and take the pressure off of Claire."

I saw his point and I called Ruby on her cell.

"David, where are you?" You don't need to know. All you need to know is that I have the rest of the week off so you can quit bothering them at the office."

"David please, we need to talk."

"No Ruby, you feel the need to talk to me, but I don't – repeat, *don't* – feel the need to talk to you, nor do I have any desire to hear what you have to say," and I hung up on her.

I spent the rest of the day looking for an apartment, finding a nice one, and playing eighteen holes of golf. The next day I moved in, hit a Wal-Mart for what I needed to set up housekeeping and then played some golf. Friday, Saturday and Sunday I worked out at the health club in the morning and played golf in the afternoon. My cell phone went off almost every hour on the hour and the caller ID always said it was Ruby – I always did not answer.

***

Monday morning, when I arrived at work, Ruby was parking in my assigned parking space waiting for me. I parked in a visitor's spot and headed for the door, but she beat me to it.

"David, we are going to have to talk sooner or later and you might as well understand that I'm fully prepared to create a scene here, follow you into the building and then to your office and do the same. I will follow you to movies, restaurants, wherever until you talk to me. I'll also call your office every ten minutes until Charlie gets so sick of it that he will order you to talk to me. Why not save everybody else the hassle and just get it over with?"

I gave in. "All right Ruby, go ahead and talk."

"Not here, David."

"Here is where I work Ruby and upstairs here is where I'm expected to be in a couple of more minutes."

"Alright, after work, come home and I'll fix us a nice dinner and after that we can have a martini and talk."

"Sorry Ruby, I'm not going back into that house and a restaurant or a bar is out of the question because I'm liable to lose it, and public scenes are just not my thing. You be here at five when I come out and we can talk in either your car or mine," and then I pushed past her and went up to my office.

She was waiting for me at five when I came out of the building. I got in her car with her and she handed me a large envelope.

"What's this?"

"Read it."

I couldn't. It was all medical mumbo jumbo and I told her so. She took it back and leafed through it and pulled out three sheets of paper and handed them to me. "Look at the dates when you read them."

The first was dated March 14, 1983. I did some quick mental arithmetic and she would have been thirteen at the time. I still didn't understand most of it, but the words *acute nymphomania* came up at me and down at the bottom of the page was a notation that the '*condition could be best treated by*' and it gave the name of some unpronounceable drug.

The next one was dated five years later, said basically the same as the first, stated that since Miss Markowitz refuses to use (unpronounceable drug), the only option open is to perform a hysterectomy; and while that option has no better than a 50/50 chance of correcting Miss Markowitz's condition, it was never the less recommended by the undersigned.

The third one was dated one week before our wedding and said the same thing that the other two had said. I handed them back to her. She put the papers back in the envelope and then looked at me. "I can't help it David. I have to have sex or I go crazy. It started with puberty and it hasn't stopped since. The only treatment is (unpronounceable drug) and I refuse to take it because it turns me into a zombie. The only other thing they can suggest is a hysterectomy and, if I go that route, I'll never be able to have babies. And I want babies David, I really do. Every year I go back to the doctors hoping that they have found a cure or at least a reasonable way of controlling it, but so far they haven't. And if I can't control it I can't have babies."

She saw the look on my face and read it instantly. "Because I couldn't be sure that they were yours," she continued. "I want babies David, but I want to be sure that the father of them is the man I love." We were both quite for a minute and then I said, "Don't you think that you should have shared this with me before we got married?"

"If you had known, would you have married me?" The look on my face must have answered that one because before I could answer, she said, " You see? I tried not to drag you into this mess, David. I knew what would happen and that's why I started all of those horrible fights in college so we would split up. I fucked other guys and made sure that you knew so you would be disgusted with me and hate me, but I loved you and I couldn't stay away from you and we always managed to come back together. I know it was selfish of me to keep my secret from you, but I couldn't bear the thought of being without you."

I sat there in the car looking at her but saying nothing; and while I had no idea what she expected me to do, I could see in her changing face the resignation that whatever it was, it wasn't going to happen.

"That's it baby. I just wanted you to know. There have been

hundreds of men in my life David, but you are the only one I have ever loved," and she started crying.

"Go! Please just go."

***

The next two months were miserable. Work kept me occupied during the day, but the nights alone in my apartment were bad. I tried dating, and while the women I dated seemed to have a good time, I didn't. I couldn't help but compare them to Ruby and they always came up short. Ruby made no further attempts to contact me, and even though several times I reached for a phone to call her, I never followed through. Neither of us had called a lawyer, at least I hadn't. I don't know if she did or not, but I never heard from one. I hadn't done it because I didn't want the hassle, and the only reason that I could see for getting one would be so I'd be free to marry again, and that was most definitely not in my near or even distant future. Once was enough for me.

I was staring at the wall, trying to work through a problem I was having with one of my projects, when all of a sudden something snapped in me. I grabbed my coat and headed out of the office. There were two cars in the driveway when I pulled up in front of the house; and even though I couldn't remember if they were the same ones that had been there last time, I still knew their significance. I entered the house to hear what I'd heard the last time and then I walked up the stairs. I took a deep breath and entered the bedroom. She was on her knees and was taking one guy from behind while she sucked off the other. They still hadn't noticed me, so I cleared my throat and said, "Excuse me. Sorry to interrupt, but I'm claiming my rights as the husband."

The two guys looked at me in alarm while Ruby froze. Her head stopped bobbing up and down on the guy's cock, but she didn't take her mouth off of it, she just stopped – frozen in place. I pointed at the guy in her mouth and said, "You're okay," and then I pointed at the other guy. "If you can get your nuts off by the time I get undressed, you're okay too, but if you can't you're going to have to make way for me until I'm through and then you can come back." He went back to slamming into Ruby while I slowly undressed. Ruby took her mouth off the guy's cock and turned to look at me with a look of disbelief on her face.

"Don't look at me," I said, "He's the one who needs your attention."

It was a long afternoon and an even longer night. The three of us took turns fucking Ruby and we did things that I'd only heard about. At one point all three of us were in her at the same time and she was screaming in pleasure. When the two guys were gone and Ruby and I were lying in bed together, she said, "Welcome home lover. Are you here to stay or just passing through?"

I rolled over on top of her. "Ask me in the morning," I said as I began the first of many couplings that would take place that night.

In the morning I awoke to the smell of hot coffee and found Ruby waiting for me when I came down stairs. In the past twenty-four hours I had come to realize that my life sucked without Ruby; but at the same time I knew that living with Ruby was going to be difficult, unless I could accept the fact that I wasn't going to be the only man fucking her. We talked and reached an accommodation. I wouldn't come home during the day anymore without calling ahead. She in turn would see to it that at least once during the week one or two of her lovers visited at night after I got home from work to help me get used to things (I have to admit that I did enjoy the previous evening.)

The coming weeks and months are going to very interesting – and maybe even a little exciting.

End of the 9th Story

Role Playing With Kirsten

I suppose you could say that I was naïve and maybe even that I should have seen it coming, but I didn't. It just happened. I thought that I was strengthening my marriage when actually what I was doing was weakening the fabric that would eventually let it disintegrate.

***

It started innocently enough. I came home from work one night to find Kirsten waiting just inside the door that connected our attached garage to the house. She was dressed in what she referred to as her 'come fuck me' suit. It consisted of a pair of thigh high nylons and a pair of high heels.

"Here or in the bedroom?" I asked as I dropped my briefcase on the floor.

"Here. I've waited long enough," she said as she climbed up on the kitchen table. "Hurry baby, I need it, I need it bad."

I unzipped, took out my cock and moved up to her as she spread her legs wide and planted both feet on the table. She pushed herself up to meet my thrust and cried out "Oh yes" as I plunged into her. It wasn't the first time that the kitchen table had been used that way and the same thing happened that always happened – the table moved every time I pushed into her and eventually the table ended up against the wall. It was great; Kirsten and I always had great sex. When I'd cum, Kirsten told me to hurry up and get my clothes off and she'd meet me in the bedroom.

"I promise you that I'll be able to get you up again."

As I peeled my clothes off, I knew what the occasion was. Kirsten always got like that when she spent the afternoon with her sister Beverly. I was of mixed minds over her afternoons with her sister Bev. On the one hand, I loved the way she was when she came home; she would not leave me alone until I was flat ass exhausted. On the other, Bev filled her head with so much off the wall bullshit that it drove me absolutely crazy.

I didn't really like Bev. She was beautiful and sexy, but she was a slut. She had worked her way through four husbands in six years and every divorce came about for the same reason – Bev's infidelity. She was a cock crazy slut and I was always uncomfortable when I knew Kirsten was going to spend time with her. Bev never tried (at least that I know of) to get Kirsten to go out and play with her, but Bev told Kirsten about everything she did; and she made it sound so great that I was afraid that someday Kirsten might want to see for herself. And that was a big worry for me because by her very nature, Kirsten was a very sexual person.

Some of Bev's talks with Kirsten were responsible for our great sex life. We were both virgins when we married, and for the first six months of our marriage it was strictly missionary position; five or six times a week, two or three a night – but always missionary. Then Kirsten came home from Bev's one day and said:

"Why don't we try this? Bev says it's great," and so doggie style was added to the mix. Next came oral and then anal followed by sexy lingerie and 'come fuck me' pumps. I had a lot to thank Bev for, but the flip side of the coin for me was that if she could talk Kirsten into trying all of those things, what else could she talk her into trying?

***

The next day at breakfast, Kirsten asked me:

"Honey, are we a normal couple?"

"I don't understand the question."

"You know, are we like other people?"

"In what way?"

"Oh I don't know. I sometimes wonder if our sex life is the norm or are we different in some way."

Aha, I thought, Bev's been at it again. "How could we know? I'm not going to go around asking people about their sex lives to try and establish a baseline."

"Don't you ever talk to the guys at work about sex?"

"Yeah, but we don't go into specifics. Mostly we just all agree that we like it and want as much as we can get. Why? What great idea has Bev planted in your mind this time?"

"She was telling me how much role playing can boost excitement in a marriage."

"Honey, Bev's experience with marriage is not necessarily something you can use as a yard stick."

"I know, but some of the things she told me about excited me just to hear about them, let alone thinking about doing them."

"Like what?"

"Like going out some night and letting me go into a bar alone, and then you come in ten minutes later and pretend to pick me up. Things like that."

"Sounds harmless enough. I suppose we could try it if you would like to."

"Can we honey? Can we do it this weekend?"

When I got home from work Friday, Kirsten was putting on the finishing touches of her outfit. She had on a black mini dress, nylons and a pair of black high heeled pumps. She finished her makeup while I took a shower and then we headed for a lounge on the other side of town where we didn't expect to run into anyone we knew. In the parking lot she leaned over and kissed me and gave my cock a squeeze.

"Give me five minutes baby. Don't wait too much longer than that or someone might beat you to me."

I watched her walk toward the front door and I wondered what I was letting myself in for. I gave Kirsten five minutes and then went inside. As soon as my eyes adjusted to the light, I saw Kirsten sitting at a table next to the dance floor and there was a guy standing there talking to her. It wouldn't fit the plan if I walked over and interrupted, so I grabbed a seat at the bar and watched. By the time my drink had arrived Kirsten had gotten up from the table and had moved out onto the dance floor with the guy.

Kirsten never looked my way as she danced to two songs with the guy. At the end of the second song the man walked Kirsten back to her table and they talked for a minute or two. Then I saw Kirsten shake her head "no" and the man left her and walked back to a table where he sat down with two other guys. I picked up my drink and swiveled on my stool to go and make my move, but before I could get off my stool, another guy was there. It took three guys and forty-five minutes later before I could get to my wife.

"What took you so long? I was afraid I might have to leave with one of them."

"Had to wait for an opening sweetie. I couldn't just come over and butt in and not make it look right. Do I just sit down or do we dance first?"

"We dance first, have one more drink and then you have to get me out of here and fuck me. I'm hot honey, and the parking lot is not out of the question. I've had cocks poked into my leg and hands on my tits and ass since we got here."

And that's just the way it was. Once in the parking lot, Kirsten had her head in my lap and she stopped blowing me just long enough to tell me to quickly find a dark place to park.

"I need it honey, I need it bad and I can't wait long enough to get home."

We fucked twice on the back seat on a dark side street and then she sucked on my cock the rest of the way home. Once in the house, she spent the next three hours destroying me.

***

For the next month we repeated the experience every Friday night in a different bar and always with the same results. Each weekend was different only in the amount of time that Kirsten wanted me to wait outside before coming in. By the fourth week, she was having me wait an hour.

"That way you don't even have to buy me a drink. By then I'll have been poked, prodded, groped and felt up enough that I'll want to fuck on the dance floor."

That night when I went in, I didn't see her. I looked for almost five minutes and I was just on the edge of panic when I saw her coming from the hallway to the rest rooms. She didn't head for a table, but walked right by me and out the front door. I turned and followed her, and as soon as I was outside, I saw her running for the car. When I got there she was already on the back seat and pulling her panties off.

"Get in here. Hurry damn it, get in here now."

Two strokes of my cock was all it took to give her an orgasm and then she screamed – actually screamed – "Fuck me damn you, fuck me hard, make me cum, make me cum."

She had one more orgasm before I got my rocks off and then she cried out, "Get me home baby, get me home before I grab some guy off the street."

Her head was in my lap all the way home, and when we got there, she ran into the house shedding clothes and crying out, "Hurry baby, hurry."

I'd already cum twice that night (once when I'd first gotten home that night and then again in the bar parking lot) so it took me a while before I was able to climax again. I think that was okay as far as Kirsten was concerned; I think she was hoping that I would go all night. Lord knows I tried just as he knew I couldn't.

After I came and fell breathless next to her, I asked her what the hell had happened that we had to rush out of the bar, and she told me. She had danced with several guys, one of them three times, and then she had gotten up to use the bathroom. When she came out, the guy she had danced with three times had been waiting for her. He had picked her up and pushed her against the wall and had shoved his tongue down her throat. Before she knew what was happening, he had managed to get her skirt up to her waist, and hand down into her panties and two fingers into her pussy. She had no idea what might have happened had not two women come down the hall and threatened to tell the manager if "You two don't take your filthy spectacle outside." The man had set her down, grabbed her hand and headed for the back door, but she broke away from him and had gotten the hell out of the bar.

"I guess that puts an end to that," I said.

"Why? I just have to make sure that I stay out in the open and don't go to the bathroom until you come in."

I couldn't dissuade Kirsten and we did it a couple of more weekends with me becoming more and more leery of what we were doing.

***

Then Bev came to my rescue, if you could call it that, by planting another idea in Kirsten's head.

"It's perfect honey, I don't even have to dance with anyone. All I have to do is play act and talk to them."

The new role play situation would be that Kirsten would pretend to be a prostitute. She would make herself look like a tramp and walk the streets downtown while I kept an eye on her from nearby doorways. She would flirt with the guys who pulled up in cars and tried to proposition her, lead them on as far as she could, and then say, "No thanks sport; you smell like a cop to me," and then she would walk away. When she got good and charged up, she would signal me and we would go home and fuck until I dropped from exhaustion.

This went on for a couple of months; but even though some nights were a huge turn on for Kirsten, like the times a guy would actually take out his cock and show it to her, most nights were 'ho-hum' and Kirsten eventually grew tired of it. We went back to the bar routine, but I obviously wasn't into it; Kirsten noticed and after a couple of weeks we stopped. Once again Bev came to my rescue.

"Would you feel like a sissy if I acted dominant?"

Oh God, what had Bev come up with now? "What are you getting at?"

"Bev says that some people can get turned on by the woman bossing the man around. Could we try that some weekend?"

"What are you talking, whips and chains?"

"No, not that. The man is a wimp and the woman treats him like one, makes him paint her toe nails, clean house, do laundry and things like that while she sits around and bosses him."

"I won't wear a dress!"

"An apron maybe?" And so began my weekends of servitude. The first weekend, Kirsten pushed me out of bed and told me what she wanted for breakfast, "And make damned sure that you don't break the yokes on my eggs."

"Yes dear," I replied as I got out of bed and headed for the kitchen.

Five minutes later she came into the kitchen and looked around. "Don't you have the coffee ready yet?"

"I put it on dear, but you know it takes a good ten minutes to perk."

"Then you need to get up ten minutes earlier tomorrow."

"Yes dear."

Then for the rest of the day it was "Donald do this" or "Donald do that" and nothing I did was to her satisfaction. It was no big thing in that everything I did was stuff that I would have done anyway, but her constant harping and bossy attitude were starting to get to me. By bedtime I was ready to tell her to stuff the role playing, at least the bossy woman part anyway. I decided to let her have that weekend and then we wouldn't do it anymore. At least, that was my plan – until we went to bed.

When I finished brushing my teeth and walked into the bedroom, Kirsten was already in bed and she was lying there with a pillow under her ass. Her legs were spread wide and she looked over at me and said:

"Well come on. Get over here and eat my pussy. At least that is one thing that I know you can do a halfway decent job of."

"Yes dear," I said as I got on the bed and set out doing what she wanted. It was a wild night. Kirsten was in total charge and she was behaving in a way I'd never seen before. She told me what she wanted done every step of the way and ordered me to do it.

"That's enough pussy licking, now I want you to fuck my ass. Try to make that little cock of yours make me scream."

When I came, she said, "Go wash that filthy little thing and then come back here and be quick about it."

She put me through the wringer that night and Sunday night, and by the time I fell asleep on Sunday I wasn't minding her bossy ways at all.

***

Kirsten woke me Monday morning with a state of the art blow job and then sent me off to work well fucked. The rest of the week was more of the same. I don't understand why, but Kirsten's weekend of being bossy had somehow charged her up sexually and the results had carried all through the week.

The following weekend started off with Kirsten pushing me out of bed to go and fix her breakfast. Then she led me to the laundry room.

"You will be doing the laundry from now on and this is the way I want it done."

She showed me how to separate the clothes, told me what soap to use, what batches needed bleach added and what water settings to use.

"When you are done with the laundry I want you to vacuum the living room. Do a good job and I just might – only might – let you in my bed tonight."

That night she damned near destroyed me. We slept in on Sunday and Kirsten woke me with a blow job and then sent me off to fix her breakfast. After breakfast I was told to run her a bath and then while she soaked in the tub, she had me fetch and carry. "Go downstairs and get me…," "Scrub my back," "Go and get me some orange juice," and on and on and on. When she was out of the tub and had dried off she told me she was ready for me to do her toe nails. She handed me the polish she wanted me to use and when I was done she looked at them and said:

"Not a bad job for the first time."

There was more bossing for the rest of the day and that night she ruined me again and the sex continued through the week. Once again I debated putting an end to this kind of role playing, but this time it was to take the pressure off of *me* – Kirsten was fucking me to death!

***

Two more weeks went by and then one Saturday evening Kirsten grabbed her purse and headed for the door.

"Where are you off to?"

"Not that it is any of your business, but since it is obvious that you can't keep up with me sexually, I've decided to go out and find you some help," and then she was out the door and gone. What the fuck, I thought, has she gone off the deep end? An hour later she was back carrying a brown paper bag.

"My lover is going to fuck me now. If you want to watch you may, but I will expect you to suck his goo out of me when he is done," and then she went up to the bedroom. I finished what I was doing and then I followed her up. She was naked on the bed and fucking herself with a dildo. When I walked into the room she took the dildo out, squirted some KY Lotion into her pussy and then went back to work with the fake cock.

"That's it lover, that's it. Show my wimp of a husband how a real man does it."

She kept that up for several minutes and then took the dildo out to give herself another shot of KY. She inserted the rubber dick in her pussy again, gave it about six strokes and then took it out and set it aside.

"Get over here and clean his cum out of my pussy. Do a good job and I may just let you use your dinky little dick for a while."

Dinky little dick? It was a good thing I was secure in my manhood or we could have had a problem there, but the weekend was another wild one; so what, did it matter.

***

Over the next couple of weeks there were some subtle changes in Kirsten's behavior. She was trying the bossy bit occasionally through the week and again my attitude was "so what, it isn't hurting anything" so I let it slide. And then she sand-bagged me and I let her get away with it. It was a Sunday afternoon and I was in the living room running the vacuum cleaner, when Kirsten came into the room with her sister Bev. I saw Bev's eyebrows go up when she saw me cleaning the room while wearing the little apron that Kirsten insisted that I wear. Kirsten said:

"When you are done with that, Bev and I need our toes done. We will be upstairs in the bedroom."

I finished the living room and went upstairs. Kirsten had me wash and dry their feet and then while they talked, I polished their nails. When that was done, Kirsten informed me that Bev would be staying for dinner and that they would like to eat at five. I said "Yes dear" and headed back down stairs. We had already decided that we were going to have barbecue steaks for dinner, so it shouldn't have been any big deal, but by the time I fired up the grill I was fuming. It was one thing for Kirsten and me to role play, but it was something else to bring someone else into the house and embarrass me.

The girls talked while we ate and I was pretty much ignored. When they did chose to include me in the conversation, I was pretty much limited to "yes dear" and "whatever you say dear." Bev stayed until ten and when she was leaving, I saw her give me a look of pity or maybe even disgust and it didn't set well with me. As soon as the door closed behind Bev, Kirsten said:

"Time for bed. Since my lover couldn't come by today, I guess I'll have to settle for you. Try not to disappoint me too much."

Three hours later, Kirsten was still trying to get me hard again as I fell into an exhausted sleep.

***

The following Tuesday was when it all went to hell. I had bottled up my anger at what Kirsten had done to me on Sunday and it had festered inside me all day Monday and most of Tuesday. By four o'clock Tuesday I couldn't hold it in any longer a nd I left work early to go home and have it out with Kirsten. I felt betrayed and I intended to let her know and I also was going to put an end to role playing.

The first thing I did when I got home was go up to the bedroom and take off my suit and put on something more appropriate for bumming around the house. When I came into the bedroom I found a naked Kirsten putting her dildo in the drawer of the bedside stand. The bed was messed up and there was a wet spot where the KY had leaked out of her and onto the bed. She looked surprised to see me and then she said:

"About time you got here. My boyfriend just left and I'm still horny. Get over here and eat me. Do a good job and I'll give you sloppy seconds."

What the fuck, I thought, I'd better do it. After I finish unloading on her about what she pulled on me with Bev, I may not get any for a while, so I'd best get it now. As soon as I slid my tongue into Kirsten's pussy, my taste buds told me that something was not right. It wasn't KY I was tasting, it was cum – and it damned sure wasn't mine. Kirsten had douched when we woke up that morning and she was in the shower when I left for work. She would have had to have done a pretty shitty job of cleaning herself not to get my stuff from the night before out of her. My wife had been fucked by another man, and not too long ago, from the look of things.

I pulled back and looked up at her. She saw the look on my face and I saw a slight change come over her face and her eyes broke contact with mine.

"How long has this been going on?"

"What do you mean?"

"You know damned well what I mean Kirsten. You think I don't know the difference between someone else's leavings and KY Lotion?"

"I don't know what you are talking about."

"Oh yes you do, Kirsten." I got up from the bed and I looked down on her. "You have been fucking someone else and my question was how long has it been going on."

"Come on baby, you know better than that. I would never do something like that to you."

"Kirsten, I just tasted cum! I've eaten you enough times after having sex with you to know what sperm tastes like. I saw you douche this morning and you were showering when I left for work. If I can taste cum now, it means that someone put it there after I left for work and after you came out of your shower, and that someone wasn't me. If you didn't want to get caught, you should have fucked me first so mine would have been there and I would have never noticed. But you have so gotten into the bossy thing that you didn't stop to think and now you are busted. Answer my question."

"Honestly honey, I don't have a clue what you are talking about."

I stood looking down at her for several seconds and then said:

"All right Kirsten, I gave you a chance."

I turned and left the room and came back five minutes later with two suitcases and a garment bag. Kirsten, who was still lying on the bed, sat up and said:

"What are you doing?"

"Packing."

"Why?"

"Because I can't stay here anymore. It is bad enough that you cheated on me, but then to keep lying when you get caught is something I won't put up with. I'll find a place to stay, get a lawyer and I guess he will handle things from there."

"You can't mean that."

"Yes I do mean it, Kirsten."

She watched as I packed and when I was done, I picked up one of the suitcases and the garment bag and headed for the bedroom door then she said:

"Wait. If I tell you will you stay?"

"No. I gave you a chance and you wouldn't take it. And to be honest, even if you had, I'm not sure that it would have made any difference."

"Don't go honey, please. What I did had nothing to do with my loving you. I do love you baby, I do. You have to believe me."

"Why should I believe you now when not ten minutes ago you lied to me and kept lying to me?"

"What did you expect? If I came right out with it, the chances were 999 to 1 that you would have walked out the door. If I played the innocent and got away with it I wouldn't lose you. I don't want to lose you baby. I love you."

"The next question is if you are screwing other guys, why are you worried about my staying? Isn't that kind of conflicting? I mean, if you are going to someone else, isn't that the same thing as saying you don't care about me? Isn't that telling me that I'm not getting the job done?"

"No, it doesn't mean that at all."

"Then why are you doing it?"

"I don't know. I mean I know why, but I don't know why."

She saw the look on my face and went on, "I know it sounds stupid, but that's the way it is. The reason I did it is because it was exciting, deliciously wicked and exhilarating and when I did it, I felt, I don't know, like I was some great goddess of sex, but I don't know why I did. The men were not even as good in bed as you are, but there was just something about it that was like a drug to me."

"The men? Not a lover or a boyfriend, but men?"

"There were three of them. I sort of got passed along."

"Passed along?"

"Yes. John was the first one and when he left town, he hooked me up with Paul; then Paul got married and he put me together with Greg."

"Just how in the hell did you get started with John in the first place?"

"I was kind of like, raped."

"How can you be kind of raped?"

"It happened the night that I told you that the guy pinned me to the wall when I came out of the ladies' bathroom. That wasn't true. He was waiting for me when I came out, but what happened was he grabbed me and pulled me into the men's room. He spun me around, bent me over the sink and took me standing up. He didn't even take my panties off, just pushed the crotch band aside and shoved it in me. It happened so fast that before I realized it, he was in me and fucking me. I opened my mouth to scream, but all that came out was a low moan and something tripped inside me. I was leaning on the sink with both hands and pushing back at him. At that point it would have been hard to cry rape and have anyone take me seriously.

"I was leaning on the sink and watching what was happening in the mirror and I couldn't believe the lust I saw on my face. He was treating me like a ten dollar whore who you would fuck leaning against the wall in an alley somewhere, and I was loving it. I had three orgasms before he came and if you remember, I was still hot when I came out of that men's room and ran for the car. Just before we left the bathroom he told me I could find him there every day after nine. I found out later that he was the owner's brother. I went back there the next day and it has been two or three times a week since then.

"Honest to god baby, I didn't know why I had to do it but I did. I came home ashamed of myself for being so weak and then spent the night loving you and thanking my lucky stars that I have you. I promise myself never again, and then as soon as you are out the door in the morning I start thinking about it, and by lunch time I'm going crazy and reaching for the phone. It consumes me and the only time it doesn't is when you are with me. I love you baby, and I'm sorry, but I never did it to hurt you or because you weren't man enough for me. It was just me being stupid and if you can just see your way clear to forgive me, I'll find some way to make it up to you. Damn it baby, I love you, I really and truly do."

"So all this role play bullshit was just a cover? To keep me too busy to find out what you were doing? Fuck poor hubby to death and he won't even begin to think I'm out running around on him?"

"No it wasn't. I was trying to make it up to you. I felt so guilty when I saw you that I just had to try and make amends. Please baby, don't leave me. I'm sorry and I'll make it up to you, I promise."

"Sorry just doesn't get it, Kirsten. Did you ever think about what you might bring home to me as a result of what you were doing? Do you have any idea of what these guys are doing when they aren't fucking you? Do you have any idea of who else they are fucking? Do the words AIDS, herpes, gonorrhea and syphilis mean anything to you? What about getting pregnant? Did you give any thought to the fact you might bring me some asshole's kid to raise? And don't tell me not to worry because you use condoms. If you used condoms, I wouldn't have tasted the last guys cum now, would I? No Kirsten, it is my life you have been fucking with and if you really loved me you damned sure wouldn't have done that. The next time you go see Bev, you can tell her that now you are as big a slut as she is. Maybe she can give you some more pointers."

I picked up the suitcase and garment bag, took them down and loaded them in the car and then went back up to the bedroom to get the other suitcase. Kirsten was lying on the bed sobbing, and for a second – only a second – my heart almost went out to her. I picked up the last suitcase and left.

The End

Here is a sample from another story you may enjoy:

JUST PLAIN BOB

HOTTEST
WIFE

EROTIC SHORT STORIES VOL. 26

For our wedding anniversary, I took Jilly to St. Thomas for a week. We swam during the day or lay on the beach, and drank and danced every night and then made love until we fell asleep. Everywhere we went, Jilly drew attention and I smiled to myself as I thought, "Eat your hearts out guys, she's mine." The third day I signed us up for SCUBA lessons, but Jilly begged off saying that she had a headache. Four hours later when I returned, she was feeling much better and wanted to make love. We skipped dinner that night and she wore me out. The next day she said that she really didn't want to go SCUBA diving and that she was just going to lie on the beach and work on her tan.

I showed up to pick up my rental tanks and found out that the compressor had broken down and that they hadn't been able to refill any tanks. They said that it would be about half an hour before they would be up and running so I spent the next thirty minutes just browsing the dive shop. Forty-five minutes later they told me that they had purchased the wrong part and that it would be at least another four hours so I headed back to the hotel. I couldn't find Jilly on the beach so I went up to our room.

As soon as I opened the door I knew what I was going to find. I could hear it out in the hall where I was standing with my hand on the doorknob.

"Oh yes, that's it, push it in. Ooh god, but that does feel good."

I quietly closed the door behind me and moved into the room where I could see the bed. Jilly was on her knees and behind her was a black man that I had seen around the hotel. He was pushing his meat into Jilly and I heard him say, "God woman, you is tight. Don't nobody get with you?"

"Not like you baby, not like you. Oh yes baby, oh yes, like that, just like that."

"How much time we got?"

"A couple of hours anyway."

"Actually," I said, "That's not quite true. Depending how you want to look at it, time either just ran out on you or you have all the time in the world from now on."

The action on the bed came to a sudden stop as both heads jerked in my direction just in time to see me turn and leave.

If you enjoyed this sample then look for **Hottest Wife.**

Also by this Author:

The Prodigal Family: The Abbotts

Watching My Shared Wife

The Waitress and the Runaway Husband

Baiting Mr. Little

Too Hot for Henry

Chuck's Fantasy

The Redhead's Desires

Rescued at Riley's

His Every Fantasy

Open Mike Night

Pursuit for Revenge

Why Does He Do That?

Halloween & Drugs

Tracey

When Rob Met Kari

Becoming a Shared Wife, Vol. 1 –
(Wife Sharing and Other Adventures)

Becoming a Shared Wife, Vol. 2 –
(Hazardous Wives)

Becoming a Shared Wife, Vol. 3 –
(Wives Who Stray)

Erotica Short Stories, Vol. 8 –

(Wild Urges)

Erotica Short Stories, Vol. 9 –

(Horny)

Erotica Short Stories, Vol. 10 –

(Stuffed Hard)

Erotica Short Stories, Vol. 11 –

(9 Shades of Sex)

Erotica Short Stories, Vol. 12 –

(Doing What She Does Best)

Erotica Short Stories, Vol. 13 –

(Hottest Nights)

A Weird One

Blackmailed MILF

Filthy Steps With My...

The Biggest She's Ever Had

Sharing Penny

Hardest Nights

My Woman's Dirty Secrets

She Makes Me...

She Needs More

My Wife's Inferno

You may also like the books by these authors:

* * *

"Why don't we go out tonight?" Adam suggested to his wife, Keri.

"If you want to," Keri agreed. "Any special reason or place in mind?"

"Actually, yes," Adam replied. "It's a special sort of place, private."

"What's it like?" Keri asked, intrigued.

"I don't really know, except that there are special costume requirements for women," Adam told her. "I heard about it at work from some of the guys."

"What kind of special requirements?" Keri asked.

"A special mask," Adam explained.

"Where do we get it?" Keri inquired.

"Well, actually one of the guys gave me one, just in case, you know," he replied lamely.

"So, let's see it," Keri said, crooking her head sideways as she looked at her husband.

Slowly Adam reached into his briefcase and withdrew the mask.

"Oh, my," Keri said, her eyes widening in surprise as she reached for it. "This is different," she commented as she held it up and looked at it. "What is this supposed to be?" she asked, indicating a mouthpiece-like part with a ball on the other end.

"You put that part in your mouth," Adam explained.

"How do you know this?" Keri asked, a twinkle in her eye.

"They showed me how it works," Adam told her. "I didn't know either."

"So show me," Keri told him, holding it out.

"Well, it's like this," Adam said, reaching up and pulling the mask over her head. It covered her eyes and nose with the mouthpiece filling her mouth. There was a good-sized hole through the mouthpiece making it possible to breath. Adam fastened the laces in the back and tightened the mask. Now Keri couldn't see or talk and Adam noticed that her breathing rate was increasing. Keri reached up with her hands and felt around the mask, feeling the soft leather and trying to control her panic at having been stricken blind and dumb in one fell swoop. When she reached behind her head for the laces, Adam quickly untied them and helped her out of the mask.

"Wow, that's some sensation," Keri said when Adam had removed the mask. "And I'd have to wear that?"

"That's the rules," Adam told her. "If you take it off you have to leave."

"Wow! It sounds really strange," she said. "Is this something that you want to do?" Keri asked him.

"Only if you want to," Adam told her. "It sounded pretty kinky to me when they told me about it."

"They've been, obviously," Keri commented. "How did their wives like it?"

"Well, he said they'd been back since, so I guess she did," Adam replied.

"Well, if you'll take good care of me I'll go and see what it's like," Keri said, smiling at him. "What else should I wear?"

"Well, I heard there's dancing, so something comfortable for that."

"It'll be strange dancing blind," Keri commented. "But it could also be sort of neat too, I guess. Let's go change," she said, turning towards their bedroom.

It only took them about ten minutes to dress. Keri wore what she usually wore to go out dancing, a short skirt and a halter top. Her full breasts filled the halter top and her skirt came only one third of the way down her thighs. She had nice long legs and she knew she looked good. Instead of her usual high heels, though, she was wearing a pair of sensible flat shoes.

"Dancing blind, you know," she said in way of explanation.

"You look great," Adam told her, meaning it.

He thought she was the hottest looking woman on the planet and he loved it when she dressed hot to go out. As they went to the car and began driving to the party, Adam was filled with trepidation. There was more about the party that he knew that he hadn't told Keri about. He'd had this secret desire for a long time and hadn't known how to act on it until now. He just hoped that Keri would go along and not freak out.

It only took them about 20 minutes to get to where they were going, a big beautiful house in the section of the city reserved for very rich people. Keri was suitably impressed as they turned into the drive and saw about a dozen other cars already parked there. When they parked, Adam pulled out the mask and held it out to her.

"Are you sure you want to do this?" he asked once more.

"Why not?" Keri asked, taking it from him. "What's the worst that can happen?"

If you enjoyed this sample then look for Naughty Swingers.

* * *

I could remember exactly when I knew my marriage to Jocelyn was over. It was the night of our tenth wedding anniversary. I came home early, brought flowers, and a nice silver pendant, that I knew she would wear. We kissed perfunctorily at the kitchen door, before I went upstairs to shower and change, prior to taking her out to her favorite restaurant for dinner.

What made it memorable is that we spoke hardly a word to each other, despite the fact that we had not seen or talked to each other since the previous evening. I typically left for work an hour before Jocelyn, and she was in the shower when I pulled out of the driveway that morning. At the restaurant, there were no reminiscences of past times together, no fond remembrances…nothing. We made the odd comment about the weather or our work, but nothing intimate. When we went to bed, I reached for her, hoping for at least some anniversary lovemaking, but she said she was too tired and that was that.

I lay on my back and knew then that it was over. We had each been pretending that our marriage was still alive. I thought back and realized, I wasn't even sure if we were ever in love with each other. We went through the motions, but I couldn't remember a moment when I knew for sure that I would do anything for her: walk through fire, slay dragons, or take on a gang of villains. It was a dispiriting thought, and with our life having sunk into ennui over the past two or three years, I knew a decision was at hand.

I delayed leaving for work the next morning. I might as well face it when I knew what I wanted to say. Jocelyn came down and was obviously surprised to see me sitting at the kitchen table with a coffee and the morning paper.

"What are you still doing here?" she asked, curious, as she poured her first coffee.

"I wanted to talk to you. It seemed like the best opportunity," I said quietly.

I suppose it was my tone of voice that alerted her. She looked at me, and then picked up her coffee, and sat in her usual chair.

"What did you want to talk about?" She was clearly uncomfortable with the uncertainty.

"Jocelyn, there's no easy way to say this. I will file for divorce early next week."

I watched her eyes grow large and heard the sharp intake of breath.

"Why?" she struggled to ask.

"I think you know the answer to that, as well as I do. Our marriage is dead. It died a long slow death, but it is dead," I said solemnly.

She sat silently, looking at me, thinking about what she had just heard. Slowly, she lowered her gaze to her untouched coffee, and stared at it for a few moments.

"I'm sorry, Lee. I wish it had worked. I'm sorry," she finally whispered.

"I know. Don't blame yourself. Sometimes … sometimes it just doesn't …." I couldn't finish the thought. I saw a tear, and then another trickle down her cheek.

"I'll look after the paperwork. If we use the do-it-yourself forms, we can cut the legal costs … unless you want to contest it," I said, almost as an afterthought.

"No … I won't fight it. You're right … it just didn't come out the way we wanted it to."

I stood up, kissed her cheek, and left quietly for the garage and off to work.

If there is such a thing as an amicable divorce, we were the model. It was civil and civilized. We split everything almost 50-50. Jocelyn's income was very healthy as an assistant director in the provincial government Ministry of Environment. Thus, there would be no alimony. We agreed to sell the house and close the mortgage. Our home in Burnaby was valued at an almost ridiculous amount, after the eight plus years that we had owned it. After we retired the mortgage, we split nearly three hundred thousand dollars. We both had our own retirement savings plans, and maintained them in our own names.

Jocelyn kept her car, but I drove a company lease car with no asset value to me. I let Jocelyn keep most of the furniture, except for a couple of pieces that had come from my parents and grandparents. I guess, all told, she would have taken away thirty-thousand or so in value more than me, but in truth, I really didn't care. I just wanted the whole unhappy episode to be over.

We met once more, just before the divorce was final, to make sure that there were no outstanding issues to be resolved. We chose a pub not far from our former residence, and found a semi-secluded place to talk. It didn't take us long to determine that there was nothing left to discuss, except our feelings and our future.

"So, where are you going to live?" she finally asked.

"I don't know. I quit my job last week. I'll be finished at the end of the month, and then I'm going to do what the Aussies do; 'go walkabout.'"

"I almost envy you. I wouldn't mind a sabbatical myself. I hope you find what you're looking for," she said sincerely.

"Me too. I just hope I'll know it when I find it. What about you … where are you going to live?"

"I've taken a job in the Ministry of Industry and I'm moving to Victoria. I found an apartment there. I'll enjoy that, I think. Less pressure than Environment."

"Good … I'm glad," I said honestly.

"Regrets?" she asked.

"Sure. Plenty. I wonder if it would have turned out differently if I hadn't been sterile. I'm sure that must have hurt you more than you let on, finding out after we were married. I know it hurt me. Not good for the male ego."

"Yes … it hurt. But then, we talked about adoption and IVF. We had choices. I'm not sure that would have made a big difference except that maybe we might have hung on a lot longer because of the kids, and then become much more unhappy. Not much of a choice in my opinion."

"I suppose you're right. Well," I said, raising my mug, "here's to a better future for us. I wish you all the best, Jocelyn."

She touched her wine glass to my mug and offered a faint smile. A few minutes later, we hugged and kissed each other for the last time. I stood and watched, as she slowly worked her way out of the pub, and into the parking lot. I slumped back in my seat, waiting for the waitress to come around so that I could order another beer. I didn't have any place special to go, and I was in no hurry to get there.

I moved in with my folks for a couple of weeks after the sale of the house. They were very generous and sympathetic. Mom and Dad were married over forty years, and I think they were deeply disappointed at my divorce. I had failed at something important, and I think they knew that I was ashamed to admit it. They said nothing directly to me, but I could tell by some of their inferences what they were thinking. The sooner I hit the road, the better off they would be.

There was only another week until the end of the month and my employment. I think they were surprised and dubious about my unplanned future, but they said nothing to discourage me. On a bright and sunny Saturday morning of March, I loaded the last of my bags into my car, kissed and hugged my folks, and drove off into the sunrise. I had absolutely no idea where I was going, but I really wasn't worried about it.

If you enjoyed this sample then look for Casual Encounters.

* * *

After the lunch crowd had gone, Anne Bernard watched Mom from the window of the diner until she got to the house. Minutes later, Mom called that she was lying down.

Mom had handled the diner for years by herself. Anne hadn't appreciated how much work it was. Even when she had helped after school, she had bitched at how hard she worked instead of seeing the killing hours Mom had worked. And, then, she'd left Mom to handle it herself for three school years while she was in college. Mom had lied to her about the cancer when she was home for Christmas, though she could tell Mom wasn't feeling healthy.

Now, Mom still came in for lunch and dinner hours. It was Molly's Diner, and Molly still kept it up.

-=-

Greg Thibault shook the cell phone in his hand. He kept from throwing it across the mesa by telling himself that that would only make the situation worse. And a worse situation than the present would be unbearable. Every arrangement which had been "of course, Professor

Thibault," or "no problem, Greg," when he had been in Boulder was unraveling at the other end of an unreliable connection.

"Look," he said, "I'll call you back in an hour or two with better reception." He punched off. He didn't know whether the guy at the department had heard him, but they would know that he wasn't on the line.

The phone companies boasted that they covered 99% of the people living in the country. This mesa was in the 1%. To be fair to the phone companies, not that Greg felt like being fair to any phone companies right then, the Anasazi weren't actually *living* in the United States. The last of them had been dead five centuries now.

He gave elaborate instructions to his students, descended by the footpath, and headed out in his Jeep. He took a quarter hour to get to something paved. The Jeep was supposed to be an off-the-road vehicle. It's just that the mesa was further off the road than the Jeep had been designed for. He found that his AC was dead, but he would have to climb back up the mesa and down again to get the keys for another vehicle. He opened the windows and got hot, moving air.

He wondered vaguely just why he'd bothered with giving the directions. Being a programming executive described as "like herding cats." Supervising archeological graduate students was like that, but worse. Everybody knew how to do the job better than the instructor did.

The nearest cellphone tower was between the two small towns of Randolph and Copper City. Randolph, the closer one, was more than an hour away. Even so, he passed only three cars on his way. Archeology got done in dry, empty country. It wasn't that Minnesota hadn't had cultures living in the area for millennia; it was that most of their artifacts had rotted or sunk into the ground. When the Anasazi had tossed out a potsherd, it was still where they'd tossed it.

He pulled into the parking lot of a diner in Randolph and called again. His hassles had only begun, and he spent half an hour on the cell, mostly on hold. By then, sweat was running down his body and pooling in the seat of his pants.

Hot, still air was worse than hot, moving air. And the air down here was, if anything, hotter than the air on the mesa. He looked across at Molly's Diner. He had seen the air conditioner when he'd driven in. His glasses were too streaked with his sweat now, but he could hear it when he listened. He'd been an idiot. He would go in and ask to make the other calls from there.

He'd left before lunch. He hadn't missed much. Assigning cooking duties only to coeds would be arrant sexism. On the other hand, guys who were going to major in Anthro didn't take home-ec in high school. Most girls who were going to major in Anthro didn't take home-ec either. Or, if his present students had, they had forgotten everything they'd learned in that course.

The diner had an air conditioner. He could hear it. He'd eat and make the rest of his calls from there. He headed into the diner.

-=-

Anne didn't recognize the customer who came in. The non-local customers were truckers. How had an 18-wheeler got into the lot without her hearing it? The guy looked rugged, but not like a trucker, and she didn't know why for a minute. Then she did. He was tanned, deeply tanned, but the tone was even. Truckers had more tan on the left side.

She grabbed a menu, and the guy sat at the counter. She got behind the counter and handed him the menu. He took off his glasses and held the menu close.

"The home-made chile looks good," he said. "Might I have some of that?"

"Coffee?"

Greg shivered, and it wasn't the AC. That voice was the sexiest voice he'd ever heard. And she wasn't trying to be sexy. She had only asked if he wanted coffee.

"Please."

Anne poured him his coffee before getting the chile. Truckers, and many locals, were more interested in the coffee than in the food. She'd learned to brew good coffee. That meant pouring out a lot and alternating pots and scrubbing them often. A cup of coffee brought in more than making a pot cost, though, and truckers chose to stop based on the quality of the coffee.

Greg liked the coffee. The chile was the best-tasting food he'd had since he'd come to the mesa. Better than that, it tasted good. He got a napkin out of the dispenser and wiped off his glasses. The waitress was the sexiest woman he'd ever seen. And it was neither her attitude nor her clothes.

She was wearing a blouse that covered her to the elbows and an apron over that. He'd spent the last two weeks with girls wearing shorts and halters, and none of them had been so attractive. The waitress had long hair, but it was tied up in a bun with a pencil stuck in it.

She hadn't presented the bill, but he paid with a $20. She brought him back his change. She stayed within sight while he ate, and that was easy on the eyes.

"Look, ma'am," he said, "the air is out in my Jeep. I have some calls to make from this area. I've been working in a dead zone." He held up his cell. "Would you mind if I made them from that table back there?"

Anne said, "Go right ahead. Want more coffee?"

"Please." This guy had said please more often to her in the last ten minutes than some regular customers had in the last month. She couldn't figure him. He didn't have a local accent. Something in his speech reminded her of the professors at Tempe, though they hadn't been that polite. He looked like he sweated every day in the sun, and he sounded like he spent his life in a library.

He stood at the counter until she had refilled his cup. Then he carried it to a table by the door. By the air conditioner, too, she noticed.

He talked on his cell. He'd been right that he had *some* calls to make. After the second, he drained his cup and put it down. She carried the pot to his table to refill the cup.

"You didn't have to do that," he said. "I could have gone back for it."

"I wait tables."

"And cook?"

"And sweep the place out at night," she said. "This place barely supports Mom and me. It couldn't pay for a big staff." How barely it supported them, she wasn't going to tell a stranger, however nice he talked.

"Well, I don't know about the sweeping, but if you cooked that chile, you did a damned fine job."

"Why, thank you."

A trucker came in for coffee and pie just then, and she didn't pay attention to the guy until the trucker was served. The guy got loud on the phone towards the end, though, and she could hear that. Apparently, he could tell.

"A lady can overhear me, which puts a real crimp in my vocabulary. But you can take the next down handbasket." The person at the other end apparently said something. "No. Both of you are women, but only one is a lady."

After he closed the cell, he brought his cup to the counter for more coffee and ordered a hamburger. He waited there for the burger, paid, and waited for his change. The driver went out and the guy went back to his table. He made another call and argued some more.

Greg was perfectly well aware that yelling on the phone didn't make them hear you any better. Sometimes, though, he couldn't resist. Finally, he ended his last conversation with Boulder and closed the cell. He brought his cup and saucer back to the counter.

"What sorts of pie do you have?"

Anne said,"Peach, apple, and cherry. We don't cook the pies, though." She couldn't figure why she'd said the last. Just that the guy had said nice things about the chile.

"I'll risk some cherry, anyway. And more coffee." She got the coffee and the pie. He paid immediately, using some of the change she'd given him earlier. She suddenly wondered whether the $20 bill was all the money he'd brought with him.

Greg ate the pie slowly. He told himself that he wanted to stay because of the coolness. The waitress was great to look at, and great to listen to, though she hardly spoke to him. Still, she was a pretty girl in a town full of young men. She was certain to be taken. He could look, but not touch.

"You were right," he said, pushing an empty plate and an empty cup away. "The pie was not home cooked. Nothing wrong with it, though. This is a nice place, how long are you open?"

That, he thought, was real suave, Thibault, not! 'When do you get off?' Indeed. The question isn't when she gets off, but where you get off.

"We're open six to ten."

"Thanks." He put a couple of bills under the edge of his plate and walked towards the door. "Really, thanks for everything," he said before going out. It would be a long drive back, and into the setting sun, too.

Anne said, "You're welcome," in a voice which was probably too low for him to hear. Then she got his dishes, spoon, and fork into the soaking water. There wouldn't be many customers before supper. She might as well wash the dishes now, so she did.

She put the tip into the cash register. About half the truckers and a quarter of the locals tipped. Their tips seldom folded. Of course, the guy had eaten a lot, and he had asked about making calls from here. But people called on cells from the diner all the time. Two free refills weren't a lot, and he sure hadn't made her walk. She did hear his car leave, though she hadn't heard it arrive.

Well, she'd tell Karen about the mysterious stranger in September, and she would invent one of her marvelous stories to explain him. Then Anne stopped smiling. Would she go back to school in September? Would she ever see Karen again?

If you enjoyed this sample then look for Molly's Daughter.

* * *

HIRED FOR
Their Pleasure
A LATE BLOOMER'S 1ST TIME

JACK RYDER

"Mom was right, you have a gorgeous body," her voice startled me awake. I guess I must have stirred a bit when my body felt the pressure of someone sitting down on the bed next to me. I was still a bit groggy as I open my eyes to see Katie sitting there staring down at me. It took a few moments for to remember that I was completely naked. I instinctively reached to pull the blankets up but found that they had been kicked off onto the floor at some point in my sleep.

"Should I lock the door from now on, or is it acceptable for me to be naked every time you barge into my house unannounced?" My voice was hoarse and strained. I could see a look of lust on her face as she gawked at my flaccid prick. "You can be naked any time I come over," she told me with her eyes never leaving my dick. "Besides, Mom told you I would be over for breakfast." I glanced at the clock and it was ten after 9am.

"Do you think I'm pretty, Jake?" She whispered. "Oh hell yes, Katie...you are so very sexy," I told her as I felt a slight wiggle. Kathleen was wearing that tiny white bikini again. The way she was seated with one leg dangling off the bed and the other leg bent beside her, left her legs spread wide apart and I could see her pussy lips pressed tight against the crotch of her bottoms.

"But, I'm so skinny and I have no tits," she complained softly. "Even Stevie has bigger tits than I have," she lamented. "Are you kidding me?" I chuckled. "With that sexy slender body, those perky cone shaped tits are perfect." I gasped. "There are many men that prefer perky tits rather than the big globe type," I informed her. "You are incredibly sexy just the way you are, sweetie."

"Do you think you could like these as much as my mother's?" Katie reached up and untied her top so it fell forward to expose her breasts to me. "Ooooh Katie, look at you," I gasped as she reached back to undo the other string and her top fell off. Her small 32A cone shaped tits were less than a foot from my face. Her pink puffy nipples were exactly the same as her mother's but seemed more pronounced since her tits are more cone shaped. She also had those pure white triangles from her bikini tan line that has always aroused me deeply. "Damn, those are sexy," I gasped.

My dick had become fully rigid within seconds as I gazed at her exposed tits. "I see you're telling the truth," she giggled as she watched my dick bouncing against my belly. "You can touch them if you like," she whispered as she scooted a little closer and pulled her other leg up onto the bed. My hands were trembling noticeably as I reached forward to fondle both of her nubile little tits.

"That feels wonderful, Jake," she purred softly as she arched her back to press her breast firmly into my hands. I let go of her left breast and used placed my right hand around her waist so I could pull her forward. "Yes Jake, Yessssss," she moaned as I wrapped my lips around her left puffy pink nipple and began to gently suck on it.

I felt her moving slightly and then felt her right hand wrapping around my rigid prick. "It's so big," she cooed when she saw that she could barely get her hand all the way around my girth. "Oooh, God Yes," I moaned as she started to gently stroke up and down my shaft. "So good,

Jake, it feels s-o-o-o-o good," she gasped when I moved my mouth to suck on her other nipple.

My legs were quivering on the bed as she slowly jerked me off while I feasted on both of her perky tits. "I was so hard for you yesterday," I confessed as she got me closer and closer to orgasm. "You made my meat so wet when you were modeling those clothes," she answered me with a moan.

If you enjoyed this sample then look for **Hired For Their Pleasure.**

* * *

Thirteen years ago I joined a private dungeon group in Seattle, Washington and had attended several parties held there and had never met anyone like Mistress. It was a Friday night and the theme that night was take down play. I am not sure if you know what this type of play involves. In a nutshell, anything goes in this play. It is usually reserved for the most extreme playing or to teach someone a lesson that was not learned before.

I had a chance before to play with others as I come to the dungeon alone and the scenes always drew an audience. You see, I love pain...cannot get enough of it. It does not matter to me what is done as long as nothing is broken and I do not require a trip to the emergency room after playing. So the scenes I was involved with became quite messy with my blood from being whipped or having needles stuck into my most private spots and various other tortures I endured.

Tonight as before, I sought out the Events Director and told her I would like to play if someone was looking. I wandered about the room watching subs and slaves being put through their paces...hearing their screams...the sounds of whips and canes striking their flesh. I do not see many males here tonight and I like that as it meant I might have a better chance at the rough playing I needed.

My wandering brought me to the far corner of the dungeon where a very pretty woman about 33 was strapped face down upon a sawhorse type of apparatus with her wrists and ankles secured tightly along the legs of the horse. There were 2 men at each end of her, one ramming her ass and the other pumping her mouth with a steady rhythm going. There was a woman wearing a black leather corset and black garter with thigh high nylons standing next to them. This woman wore no panties and had a neatly shaved vagina that peeked out from under the garter affair she wore. As the men fucked the helpless woman on the horse, the other woman was whipping her hard across her back and shoulders. Her back was crisscrossed with dozens of stripes looking very red and some almost purple. Blood oozed from many of the whip marks.

I was so enthralled by this scene I was not aware the Event Director was calling my name. I kind of jumped a little when she touched me on my shoulder and I turned to see her standing there with another woman I had never seen before. She introduced her as Miss Sarah and left us alone. This woman was beautiful with long flowing dark brown hair and deep blue eyes. She had an ample bosom, tight waist, long, shapely legs. The most striking thing about her was the long elegant evening dress she was wearing. More suited to being at a fancy ball then a dungeon. Miss Sarah had been watching the scene I was and had a chance to watch my reactions also. As she stood beside me she asked my name and I replied, "Miss Sarah I am David". We talked for 20 minutes while watching the whipping continue and I was asked many questions about my likes and dislikes and what I hoped to find here tonight.

I told Miss Sarah what my limits were. While I did this I looked her in the eyes and I could almost see a fire glowing from inside her. I shrugged it off as my over active imagination playing tricks on me. Miss Sarah reached her hand out and stroked my broad chest and it was almost like being touched with an electric current. It took my breath away and I felt my knees quiver just a little. I had never felt this way from being touched before now.

Miss Sarah eyed me and watched my expressions as she asked if I really wanted to play with her tonight. I almost screamed out my answer but managed to hold back and told her, "Miss Sarah I would like to play with you."

She placed her hand in mine and walked away from this scene to the various restraint sections of the dungeon until we stopped at a huge wooden X shaped thing. The beams were 10 feet long and made of solid oak 8 inches square. Each beam had 12 eyehooks bolted into it and was impossible to pull loose from the wood. The top and bottoms of the beams were secured to the roof beams and wooden floor and would not tip over no matter how hard someone would struggle.

If you enjoyed this sample then look for <u>The Mistress And The Pet</u>.

WANT FREE COPIES OF MY BOOKS?
Just visit my blog and download free copies of my books:
awesomeauthors.org/justplainbob

www.ingramcontent.com/pod-product-compliance
Lightning Source LLC
Chambersburg PA
CBHW072355190626
46811CB00019B/899